I0760587

Ex libris
C P

**Also by Amelia Littlewood**

Death at the Netherfield Park Ball

The Mystery of the Indian Diadem

The Peculiar Doctor Barnabus

The Apparition at Rosing's Park



Published by Cyanide Publishing
www.cyanidepublishing.com

First edition



This is a work of fiction. Names, characters, businesses, places, events and incidents are either the products of the author's imagination or used in a fictitious manner. Any resemblance to actual persons, living or dead, or actual events is purely coincidental.

ISBN: 978-1-9997600-6-9

FROM THE JANE AUSTEN NOVEL
*Pride & Prejudice*

# SHERLOCK HOLMES
*and*
# ELIZABETH BENNET
*Mysteries*

Volume 1

AMELIA LITTLEWOOD

CYANIDE PUBLISHING

# CONTENTS



## Bonus Content

FROM THE JANE AUSTEN NOVEL
*Pride & Prejudice*

*A Sherlock Holmes & Elizabeth Bennet Mystery*

AMELIA LITTLEWOOD

# CHAPTER ONE:
## *The Mysterious Mr. Bingley*

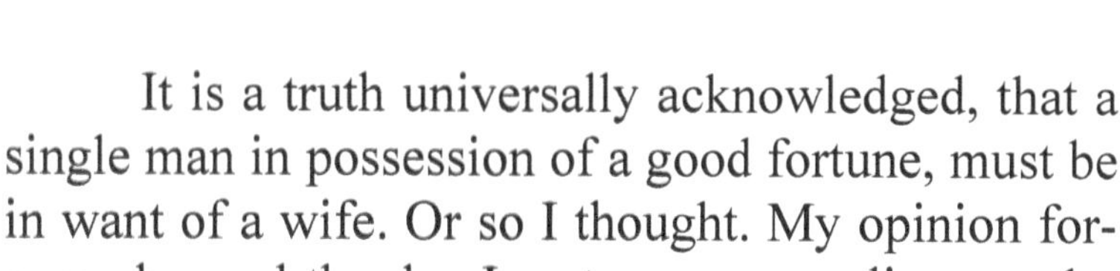

It is a truth universally acknowledged, that a single man in possession of a good fortune, must be in want of a wife. Or so I thought. My opinion forever changed the day I met a very peculiar man by the name of Mr. Sherlock Holmes.

~~ o ~~

"Did you hear?" Mrs. Bennet said, looking up from her needlework. When Mr. Bennet did not respond, she asked again. "Mr. Bennet, *my dear*, have you heard the news?"

After some time, Mr. Bennet looked up from his book. “My dear Mrs. Bennet, I have heard much news today. To which bit of it are you referring?”

“Why, the news that Netherfield Park has been let at last.”

“No, my dear, I had not heard that *particular* piece of news.”

Mrs. Bennet looked up from her needlework once more. My darling sister Jane and I shared a humorous glance.

“Do you not want to hear who it has been let out to?” she asked, eagerness in her voice.

“I suppose you will tell me no matter my response," the man replied dryly. He had been a constant companion to my mother’s nerves for near three decades. His calm demeanor was the only way he could have survived those long years.

“Why, Mr. Bennet, it has been let by a young man of large fortune!” she exclaimed.

“What is the man's name?”

“Bingley.”

“Is he single?” Although our father claimed to be above such nonsense as marrying his daughters off, he asked the question with feigned disinterest.

My youngest sister let out a gasp. She was consumed with the thought of matrimony, and in what she would claim to be love with near every eligible man she crossed paths with. It was unlikely that she would marry before myself and Jane were wed. Although all five of us Bennet girls were out in society, it would be a rather scandalous thing should our three youngest sisters be married prior to ourselves.

With simple deduction, I figured the answer to his question. My mother would not likely have shared this gossip with father were the gentleman letting Netherfield Place married.

"Single, yes, my dear Mr. Bennet, and of large fortune. Four, even five thousand a year."

Lydia squealed in excitement, gathering Kitty's hands in her own. The two danced about the room, all ridiculousness and youth.

"How lovely for our girls, do you not think, Mr. Bennet?"

"I am sure I do not know what you mean. What could this gentleman possibly mean to them?"

I stood from my chair, deciding that now may be a good time to go for a walk. I enjoyed father's teasing, but could only tolerate it for a short time. Mama's plan was surely to marry one of us to the poor, unsuspecting man and Papa knew this to be her desire. I squeezed my dearest sister, Jane's, hand before taking my leave.

I had no interest in such talk of marriage and fortune. It was intellect and human nature that interested me. As such I had resigned myself to never marrying and dying an old maid. I could not abide by a life of performing the role of an obedient and uninteresting wife.

Of my five sisters, my elder sister, Jane, was the most beautiful. In truth, Jane was more beautiful than any woman in town and she was at least thrice as kind as she was beautiful. My two youngest siblings, Kitty and Lydia were good-humored and handsome enough. Mary, next youngest to me, was stern and shy of nature and quite plain. Myself, I could not compare to Jane and often was. I was second in birth and second in fairness. I did not begrudge her this, I loved her too dearly. I had books and cleverness, as well as a sharp wit that often got me into trouble. Although I had left the conversation about the mysterious Mr. Bingley, I must admit that I was intrigued.

A mysterious and single young man of large fortune moving to the countryside did not occur often. Now if he were to be handsome as well, I would be sure he was hiding something. Not that it mattered how handsome or plain the man was, he would have the mothers of all the young unmarried women throwing their daughters at his feet. I cannot be a judge of them, although I question how so many women can be so careless when it comes to their own hearts. I suppose they are not, but simply care more for their wallets than I. If this Mr. Bingley wasn't hiding anything, then he was sure to be a fool. No reasonable man of money left the city for a town like Meryton, no matter how grand he thought Netherfield Park to be. By my mind, he would not last long here, no, he would surely get bored of the society and move on soon enough.

As I walked about the gardens, I imagined what sort of sordid past the man was running from. He was likely to be a perfectly fine gentleman with no scandals in his past. However, I preferred my version of the man. I believed him to be rather nefarious, with a penchant for gambling, opium dens, and brothels. A man of large means and many vices. Perhaps he fell into debt with a dangerous man, and as such, had to flee to the countryside for a life of boredom and relative anonymity. I often delighted in imagining such things. It was improper, and a woman of my standing should pretend to not know of things such as brothels and gambling and opium dens. It was in my nature to ignore such societal pressures, if only in my own mind. Never would I speak such things aloud; I would certainly be sealed in my fate as an old maid if I did. If he were to be a dull, handsome, kindly man, I hoped he would take a liking to my dear Jane. If there were any woman in this world who deserved happiness and a large fortune, it would be Jane.

Lost in my thoughts for quite some time, I did not realize how late it had gotten until my stomach began to ache in hunger. I had walked very near the mile to Meryton, and turned back towards home in order to keep my hunger at bay. Meryton was a small market town a mile from Longbourn, where myself and my family resided. Though small, Meryton was of enough importance to have had a mayor at one point in time. Sir William Lucas, the father of my dearest friend, Miss Charlotte Lucas, held the position. I found myself wishing that the direction of my walk had been towards Lucas Lodge, where they resided. Charlotte was a sensible and intelligent woman of near twenty-seven. She would surely be my companion in life, the two of us old maids together. Alas, I had meandered in the opposite direction and must turn back home, where I was sure to hear more of the mysterious Mr. Bingley and the certainty of which Mama spoke of his plan to marry one of the Bennet sisters.

Surely enough, when I arrived back home, the only conversation to be had was about Mr. Bingley. Papa had continued in his way to refuse meeting and becoming acquainted with the man. His teasing of poor Mama had gotten her nerves in a state. Mrs. Bennet's entire business of life was to get her daughters married to the best sort of man, as it also seemed to be the business of every other mother. If Papa should not call on Mr. Bingley then we should have to rely on the likes of Mrs. Long to acquaint us with the gentleman at the assemblies in town. Jane told me that Papa had teased that Mr.

Bingley should prefer Mama out of all the Bennet's, and as such, he shan't call upon him. He did, however, offer that when twenty men of five thousand a year come to town, he should call upon all of them. Though Mama's nerves were suffering, Kitty and Lydia were in the throes of excited and youthful imaginings of the fancy balls and parties they would be invited to once Mr. Bingley arrived, and should he marry either of them, the fancy parties they would have. It was nonsense, for if Mr. Bingley were to choose either of those silly girls over our beautiful Jane, I dare say that Papa would not consent. He would be too skeptical of the man's intentions and quite frankly, his intelligence, to allow him to marry even the silliest of my sisters.

"It is a wonderful excitement, though, do you not think, Lizzy?" Jane asked over the clamour of Kitty and Lydia. She knew my nature to be cynical of newcomers, though I am sure she would be horrified of my imaginings of the revered Mr. Bingley.

"I should very much like it if he were to throw a ball. Private balls are so much nicer than public."

"Oh, I so hope he does have a ball, it's such a nice manner of meeting people," Lydia fretted. "It's so dull here. It would offer great escape and much excitement in our lives," she said with drama.

"How is a dance a nice manner of meeting people?" Mary questioned. "Do you not think conversation is a much better manner in meeting people, in order to discover their true nature and character?"

I responded before my youngest siblings could so to save Mary from their ridicule. "It would seem so. However, it would be much less entertaining."

"I do not care for balls. I think them to be tiresome events, where nothing can be gained but making a fool of oneself dancing."

Lydia and Kitty giggled at their unfortunate sibling.

"I would be delighted if he were to have one. I think it would be great fun," Lydia said, giggling again with Kitty by her side.

"If your father refuses to call upon him, it will not matter if Mr. Bingley throws a thousand balls, for we will not be invited to even one of them," Mrs. Bennet fretted.

Although Mr. Bennet seemed to have refused to call upon the gentleman, I was certain he would become acquainted with him. He was sure to be playing a trick on poor Mama's nerves. Though he tried to appear uninterested in the marriage of his daughters, and certainly uninterested in the advantageous marriages of his daughters, he would be a fool not to care. If Papa were to die, it would leave Mama and my sisters and I at the mercy of one Mr. Collins.

Papa had no sons. Therefore, no matter how unfair it was, his property went to the next male heir, which was our cousin, Mr. Collins. Should we not secure marriages, and advantageous ones at that, our fate would be in Mr. Collins' hands. He could turn us out at any moment should he desire to do so. It would be in our best interest to marry well, as such was our position.

Should Papa want to secure our futures, he would have to advocate for the lot of us by calling upon Mr. Bingley. It would be a shame if we were to be required by circumstance to rely on Mrs. Long or the likes of which to make us acquainted with the gentleman. Mama was sure that she would not introduce us, as she had two unmarried nieces of her own.

In the end, Papa was among the first to call upon Mr. Bingley. Near a fortnight after the news that Mr. Bingley had procured Netherfield Park did he arrive. Papa refused to lend any information about the gentleman—whether he seemed good natured, was handsome, or the like. It was a dreadful tease of him to do so, but the news of his calling upon Mr. Bingley sent the house into uproar. As was custom, Mr. Bingley ought to return the call and come here to Longbourn. That begged the question of when he would arrive and how long he would stay for. Mama went into a nervous tizzy about what should be served for dinner should he stay and Lydia and Kitty were excitedly giggling and wondering if he should like their hats.

Mr. Bingley returned Papa's call only a couple days after Papa's visit. It was terrible timing, as my sisters and I, as well as Mama, were not present for his visit. He was clearly a man of good manners, or at the very least, feigned his manners well. Mama sent an invitation to Netherfield for Mr. Bingley to dine with us, but Mr. Bingley was forced to decline, as he was heading back to London. Mama's nerves went into a panic at this news. She could never marry her daughters to the gentleman should he not stay long enough for her to even attempt to pawn one of us off on him.

It was not until we visited Mrs. Lucas that we learned any details about the gentleman. As such was Papa's nature, he had little reason for shielding Mr. Bingley's nature from us. Mrs. Lucas informed us that he was a kind-natured man who was fond of dances and balls and, by all accounts, handsome. It seemed to be far too fortunate for all of us single women that such a man should move here, solidifying in my mind the man's sordid past.

She also gave us reason as to why Mr. Bingley had returned to London. As Mr. Bingley was so fond of balls, he had gone back to London to bring a large party back to accompany him at the public ball in a fortnight. Mama delighted in this news.

# CHAPTER TWO:

## *The Public Ball*

It was at the public ball where we were finally acquainted with Mr. Bingley. He and his party arrived fashionably late. His guests were as much the talk of the party as he was. Gossip about his guests had run rampant throughout town while he traveled all the way to London to gather them. Such a trip was worthy of gossip no matter who the traveler. The fact that this traveler in particular was of such wealth made the gossip all the more scandalous.

It was rumored that his party was to be near a dozen. Lydia speculated that Mr. Bingley was sure to bring all the most beautiful women in London with him. She spent days sulking, certain that none of them would ever be married to him, as he was sure to be in love with one of these imagined women that he spent time with in London. Kitty believed that his party would be full of the most fashionable women that she'd ever lay eyes on, and hoped that there would be plenty of handsome men in the party, as well.

The fashionably late arrival of Mr. Bingley and his party meant that every eye at the ball was on them. True, this would have been the case regardless, but their arrival nearly stopped the entire ball. The music was momentarily interrupted when they stepped into the meeting hall, which put a pause on the dancing, as well.

He walked in with the grandeur and attitude that should be expected from a man earned five thousand a year. The party was but four and Mr. Bingley. Two ladies and two men. The women were soon known to be his sisters, Mrs. Hurst and Miss Bingley, and one of the men his brother-in-law, Mr. Hurst.

Upon the discovery that the two women were of relation to Mr. Bingley, interest in them considerably lessened. Prior to this discovery, the opinions of the female guests of Mr. Bingley were almost spiteful in nature, but as soon as the fear of competition was proved to be false, the opinions of his sisters changed drastically.

In truth, the women appeared to be snobbish. They stood with their arms crossed and their noses upturned. It was slight, and without proper observation, I don't believe that any other would have noticed their attitudes. To me, it was clear that they were none too happy to be at the public ball, or even in Meryton at all. Should Mr. Bingley grow to love any woman in town, I suspected that at least one of his sisters would disapprove of the match.

There was nothing remarkable about the brother-in-law. He appeared to be a gentleman, maybe not very discerning or intelligent, but kind enough. He was certainly oblivious to his wife's disregard of the people of Meryton.

Mr. Bingley himself was quite handsome, and good-natured as they come. Although initially suspicious of such a man, as I met him, he convinced me he could never be the type to frequent any kind of dubious establishment or commit any such nefarious act as I imagined him capable.

The same could not be said of his other male companion, who quickly became the subject of everyone's speculation. He was clearly a strange fellow, either much poorer than his compatriots or so wealthy that his state of dress was not of concern to him. The man was handsome, but odd in more than just a singular way. He created more gossip than anyone who ever came through Meryton before him. He was in a state of disarray, completely underdressed for the occasion. His appearance was disheveled, though it did not detract from his handsome features. He was not a pleasant man, of that I was sure, too wrapped up in his own head to care for a moment about social niceties and propriety. Still, I was intrigued by him. Never had I come across such a person.

Although their entrance interrupted the merriment of the night, the interruption only lasted a few moments before all attending were once again dancing and engaging in gossip, no doubt about the new arrivals.

The new arrivals to the ball began conversing with the only people that Mr. Bingley knew well, the Lucases. It was when they were conversing with our dear friends that I first met Mr. Holmes.

Mr. Bingley easily got himself acquainted with all the important people in the room. He was kind and unreserved in manner, and enjoyed every dance there was to be had, with seemingly boundless energy. I'd wager that near half the woman who spoke with Mr. Bingley left the ball smitten with the amiable man, including the married and older women who had the pleasure of making conversation with him. He danced with Jane twice, which pleased Mama more than she could express, though she tried.

In stark contrast, Mr. Holmes danced only twice, once with Mrs. Hurst and then with Miss Bingley, though there were many women in want of a partner. In truth he appeared uncomfortable to be there, as though he felt he was better than the company, since the only woman who he deigned to dance with were within his party. It was my opinion that this was not the case, only that he did not possess the same amiable qualities as his friend, making it harder to easily converse with so many that the man was not familiar with. However, I had no cordial feelings towards him or pity for his predisposition to be unfriendly.

His behavior did not go unnoticed by the other women at the ball, and he was quick to lose favor with Mama as he insulted me directly. I sat out but two dances because of the shortness of men at the ball, and I sat near enough to Mr. Holmes and Mr. Bingley to overhear their conversation. The two men were discussing the dance, and specifically the women in attendance.

"I have never seen such incredibly beautiful women in my entire life!" Mr. Bingley exclaimed. His breath came fast. He had barely taken a moment from dancing. "You should engage in another dance, Holmes, instead of brooding by yourself."

"I have no such intention to dance," Mr. Holmes replied, taking no true offense at his friend's jibe. "I must disagree with you on your first account, though. You were engaged in dance with the only handsome woman in the room."

I felt my heart leap as the man eyed my dearest Jane and I heard Mr. Bingley agree with the statement enthusiastically. I hoped in my heart of hearts that his finding her beautiful would grow into something more. I had not seen my Jane so happy in some time as when she was dancing with Mr. Bingley. What little I knew of him, his nature seemed as though it would complement Jane's. Although Mr. Holmes said that Jane was the only handsome woman there, with I'm sure the exception of Mr. Bingley's own sisters, this was not the offending remark.

"You are too harsh, Holmes. One of her sisters is behind you now. She is quite handsome and I dare say agreeable."

I found myself flattered by the comment. I was unused to such claims. It was not often that one heard such compliments so freely given. A compliment given face-to-face was not something that could be trusted, but a compliment given when the complimenter did not know the one they were complimenting could hear must by default be the truth. I would gladly take *quite handsome* and possibly *agreeable*, especially when being compared with Jane.

"She has an interesting intelligent look about her, I'll give you that. But I am not in such a desperate rush to find a wife." He then went on to urge his friend to go back to Jane before another man gained her affection.

I shared the story eagerly and with a laugh to my friends. I delighted in all things ridiculous. Though I retold the story with a smile, it would be a lie to say I was not hurt by the comment. Charlotte Lucas knew that my smile concealed my hurt, and tried to offer me comfort, but I did not welcome her kindness, as it made me feel uneasy to speak about my feelings. I was surprised that someone could so quickly sum up my personality in a mere glance. Was I that transparent?

No one appeared to know much about Mr. Holmes - there was a deeper sense of mystery surrounding the man. No one could be sure if he came from money or not, though it was assumed he did based simply on the company he kept. With the way Mr. Bingley's sisters turned their noses up at us common folk, no one believed that either of them would sully their reputations by lowering themselves to not only associate themselves with someone of low standing, but to travel with them as well. No one seemed to know who he was, or for that matter, anything else about him at all.

It was not much later that some of his mystery was lifted. The man was not mysterious because he didn't want to share about himself. Quite the opposite, when asked a question, he responded honestly and without hesitation. His inability to engage in conversation was what shrouded him in mystery, his quiet and discerning demeanor. When someone queried where the man lived, he responded that he lived at 221 B Baker Street. This caused a flurry of reaction among the ball's guests. It was rather unusual for a man of means to live in an apartment.

"Did you hear that the strange man Mr. Bingley brought with him, Mr. Holmes, is a detective of some kind?" Charlotte informed me.

"I do not much care to hear about Mr. Holmes, clearly I am too intelligent for him, my dear Charlotte." I said dramatically, teasing my friend.

She laughed at my quip, but her expression was one of slight pity. I loved her, but begrudged her for knowing me so well. She knew all my secrets, even the ones I did not know I held. It was she who understood me better than any other, even better than Jane. Jane did not share my cynicism, and thusly could never fully know me. I did not share her optimism, so I could never truly know her. This did not change how fond we were of one another. Charlotte and I had much differing opinions, but we shared the same general outlook on life.

"Well, he's quite right. No man will look at you if your nose is always stuck in a book. I find it fascinating, and quite gruesome. Mr. Holmes solves crimes in London. He lives in an *apartment*!" Lydia said, interrupting mine and Charlotte's conversation. She and Kitty had enjoyed the company of many men and the pair of them had spent near the entire night dancing. Although they were ridiculous and silly girls, they were good-humored and their nature was such that men took interest in them. I oft worried about the two of them, Lydia more than Kitty. Both of them were too consumed by the idea of men, making us all appear as ridiculous as them. Kitty simply followed in Lydia's footsteps, mimicking her elder sister's actions. Should Lydia ever do something foolish, Kitty would likely follow.

"Do you think that Mr. Holmes has ever studied a murder case?" Lydia asked, scandalized at the thought of it.

Unfortunately for her, Mama overheard this question.

"Lydia! Mind your tongue. How could you discuss such things? And in *public*?" Mama admonished Lydia.

Should this question have been asked in private, in the comfort of our home, Mama should not have cared such or have been so upset by the question. That Lydia asked in public was her true offense. Mama cared for our public reputation, though she often forgot herself when she obliged herself too much in libations.

"Mr. Bingley mentioned that Mr. Holmes has worked a multitude of cases, but the details of which were certainly not appropriate to discuss in public," Jane said, coming upon our conversation. She was quick to end the conversation before any of my siblings were able to bring ridicule to the family. Jane was never improper. Her demeanor simply did not allow for such diversion from societal niceties.

"I am absolutely uninterested in whatever cases the man has worked. He does not dress like a gentleman or participate like Mr. Bingley. He is arrogant in nature," Mama said.

It was then that Mr. Bingley came to beg Jane for another dance, though he only need ask. Dear Mama near jumped out of her skin when he arrived, not expecting him to join the conversation at such an unfortunate point in her speech. Whether Mr. Bingley heard her hateful words or not, he gave no indication. The mischievous part of my soul hoped that he had, so that he may extend our feelings of distaste to Mr. Holmes. The politer part of myself hoped he had not heard, so to not offend Mr. Bingley himself. I should not want our shameful comments to negatively impact Jane's prospects.

"Miss Bennet, would you do me the distinct honor of joining me in this next dance?" he asked Jane.

Mr. Bingley made his request with a jovial smile. He had a strong confidence in societal conversations, something his friend lacked. Either Mr. Bingley did not have the intelligence to be concerned with the finer points of conversation nor the opinions that were formed about the man during conversation or he was simply wealthy enough that he didn't have to be concerned with such matters. Mama went from startled by Mr. Bingley's presence to incredibly pleased by it. I think Mama was even happier than Jane, her marital scheme taking such great shape so early into their meeting.

"Nothing would please me more than to take this next dance with you," Jane agreed, taking Mr. Bingley's arm as they moved to the dance floor.

Mama's face beamed with personal satisfaction as she watched them begin the dance. The woman would surely take credit for the sun rising should she be able to. Her face twisted into a scowl as she noticed the disheveled figure of Mr. Holmes to have been standing near to Mr. Bingley before he exited to the dance floor, leaving him near to us. He was scowling, as well, a face that could be compared to a thunderstorm.

"Mr. Holmes, why do you not dance? There are far more women here and the men are scarce,"

Mama prodded him, trying to goad the man into admitting that he was of the mind that he was better than the rest attending the ball.

"I do not partake in dancing often," was his response, and he spoke emphasizing every word he said. "It is a silly distraction which I cannot abide by, ma'am."

"Should you not engage in such silly distraction, as you call it, as you are in attendance at a ball? Without dance, one cannot much call it a ball, especially when so many young ladies are being dismissed so easily by the lack of men in attendance," I said with a mischievous grin.

To anyone hearing our conversation, it would sound like a simple observation of the lack of men at the dance. Mr. Holmes did not react in a chagrined or defensive manner as I expected of him.

"It is not the politest thing of me, no, but for me, dancing is not the enjoyable part of a ball."

Mama had become engaged in conversation with Miss Lucas, and Lydia had been swept onto the dance floor once again. It was really just myself and Mr. Holmes present for our discussion. He was handsome, yes, but I found him to be of very peculiar character. I was more intrigued by this odd man than I wanted to admit to myself.

"Pray, tell me, should you not enjoy dancing at a ball, what part *do* you find enjoyable?"

It surely was not the drink, as the man had not had a sip of any libations since he had arrived. I myself doubted that he had much enjoyment in conversing as he had not engaged many outside of his own party in much discourse. Aside from discussion, drink, and dance, I was curious to know what Mr. Holmes found enjoyable about a ball, as to my eye, those were the instrumental pieces to make a ball.

"Observation," he responded. "Miss Bennet, observation is my true joy in life."

"What have you observed this evening, then?"

"Lots," he said, a grin spreading across his face. "The young gentleman over there," as he nodded his head to the opposite side of the room where a young man stood, "has relieved the purses off of three unsuspecting people already, and that woman over there is almost certainly engaged in an affair with more than one of the young men in this room, all of whom are jealous of one another. Likely they will engage in a brawl of some sort later this very eve to win the fair maiden's heart."

I studied the man and the woman that Mr. Holmes indicated in his observations. I could not see anything indicating them as dubious at first. Only upon further investigation did I notice that the man Mr. Holmes indicated as a pickpocket had a rather large bulge on his lower back where he had stuffed the purses. The woman, though I never would have come to the conclusion on my own, certainly had affairs with the men she danced with, cycling through them. She was too informal with them, more comfortable and far too close with the men she was entertaining. It was incredible to see.

"How could you tell all of that from just from observing?"

"The same way that you were able to see it once I showed you the clues which you were seeing but not understanding."

I continued to look about the room. I was curious to see just how Mr. Holmes could predict that the gentlemen competing for the lady's affection would duel later in the evening. I supposed it would just be an educated guess, that the men she was pitting against one another were showing signs of tension and agitation.

"Is this how you solve crimes, Mr. Holmes?"

He was surely an arrogant man, but I supposed that with such intelligence, arrogance was easy to come by, almost a side effect.

"That is exactly how I solve crimes, Miss Bennet."

# CHAPTER THREE: The Man in the Militia

It took time for the excitement of the ball to wear off. Just as Mr. Holmes predicted, a fight broke out not long before the ball was supposed to end. It was all the town could talk about, the most exciting thing to have happened in Meryton in a long time. Combined with the excitement surrounding Mr. Bingley and his party, gossip ran rampant through the town.

Mama was at her best; gossip and matchmaking were her two callings in life. Her talents in them were unmatched by any other.

Mr. Bingley should have been the talk of the town, but he was outshone by the poor young woman's scandal. The fight was so scandalous that the young woman in question went to stay with her aunt and uncle in London. It was customary for these young ladies caught up in scandals to take some time away until society forgot. Society never really forgot, though. It might move on to another scandal, but there was no forgetting any of them. I pitied her, and her family more, for they were made to appear ridiculous and that stain should never leave them. There was no mercy when a woman besmirched her good name.

The men involved with the woman were not granted the same treatment. The gentlemen were given the freedom to go about their lives as though nothing had happened.

Mama had spent most of her time discussing how Jane and Mr. Bingley danced together twice. Mr. Bingley had not danced with any other women more than once. She was certain that these two dances meant the two should be a love match for certain. I knew both were smitten with one another, for it was not hard to tell. Jane had been all smiles since the two met, and although she was usually of this disposition, I could see that she was happier than was typical. I should hope for her a happy marriage to the gentleman Mr. Bingley, should they begin to know each other better. It was an advantageous marriage to be sure, but I dreamt that she should have a happy marriage with the man, not just with his money.

Once the excitement of the ball died down, there was new excitement to be had. The militia was coming through Meryton. Lydia and Kitty were beside themselves with glee at the thought of meeting an officer.

It came at a poor time, though, as our cousin Mr. Collins had come to join us for an undetermined amount of time. The purpose of his visit was not lost to me, as he was an unmarried man and effectively all our belongings were his. The man was here to take his pick of a wife. Should he attempt to choose Jane, Mama would surely intervene on behalf of her. She was convinced that Mr. Bingley should be making an offer of marriage to her shortly. I felt this to be hasty, but after being acquainted with Mr. Collins, I did not believe that he would be a good match for any woman, but especially not for Jane. Should Mama redirect his attentions, I worried onto whom they should turn.

Mr. Collins had dedicated himself to the church as a clergyman. He did seem more concerned with his patron, Lady Catherine, than with God, though. He was a silly man, narrow-minded and pompous. He subjected us all to speeches about God and the ways of mankind that seemed never to end. Papa was at the end of his wits listening to Mr. Collins' long-winded sermons.

The man was, according to himself, attempting to extend an olive branch to Papa. His father and my father had long ago had a disagreement that resulted in the pair of them no longer speaking. I had no inkling of the details of their disagreement, but it must have been great. There was much tension between Mr. Collins and Papa because he was the son of the man with whom Papa disagreed and he was set to inherit all our belongings. That tension was not made better by Mr. Collins' insufferable nature.

It was a nice reprieve for Papa that we had Mr. Collins join us to Meryton. It was undoubtably no reprieve for us, though. Mr. Collins was uncomfortable with going into town with us; it was silly frivolity in his eyes, and with Lydia and Kitty falling over the officers and giggling, he was most shocked by their behavior. Aside from officers, only new ribbons or hats could keep their attention. Mr. Collins' sermon was cut short by their obvious disinterest as they went from shop to shop, their attention being taken by near every new excitement in town. Mary had declined to come along, seeing no enjoyment in going to town, and as such, Papa and Mary got a much needed break from our unwelcome company.

Mr. Collins ceased his incessant speech when we came upon two handsome gentlemen that drew Lydia and Kitty's attention as soon as their eyes fell upon them. I cannot say that how handsome the gentlemen were was lost on me. Upon some conversation, we became acquainted with Mr. Denny and Mr. Wickham. They were indeed handsome, and quick in conversation. Lydia was particularly drawn to Mr. Wickham, though he seemed not to be interested in her. He directed many a question at me, though. The attention flattered me and I enjoyed our teasing discussion. I did enjoy speaking with them, but my curiosity was not particularly piqued until we met Mr. Holmes and Mr. Bingley while we were walking along the country road heading back towards our homestead. The two were on horseback, on a ride into town.

Most everything about the interaction seemed exceedingly normal, except for Mr. Holmes' and Mr. Wickham's reactions to one another. Their interaction was full of subtle intricacies. The way they posed their bodies gave the impression as though they were once acquainted with one another. Mr. Wickham's jaw tightened as the two men on horseback greeted us and the two only offered each other a terse nod in acknowledgement.

"Miss Bennet, how wonderful it is to see you again!" Mr. Bingley exclaimed. He forgot himself in only addressing Jane and quickly corrected this obvious and telling oversight. "And, of course, all the other Miss Bennets. Wonderful to see you all," he stammered.

Lydia and Kitty held back their raucous laughter, but not very well. They found humor in Mr. Bingley's eagerness to see Jane. I found some humor in his inability to hide it, but more than that, my heart soared as the two of them locked eyes and instantly lit up.

I hoped that maybe Mr. Collins would observe their interactions and not make an offer of marriage to Jane, but I did not trust his capability to understand the finer points of conversation and thusly did not believe that he would take any notice. When I turned to observe him, I found him paying no attention to the conversation at hand as he stood uncomfortably far behind the rest of the group.

"When shall you throw your ball, good sir?" Lydia quizzed Mr. Bingley before Jane could respond. She waved the ribbons that she had gotten in town about the air. "You see, I have purchased ribbons for it already, and you have promised to throw one! When shall it be?"

"Beautiful ribbons, Miss Bennet. Just smashing. The ball shall take place in haste so you do not waste your lovely ribbons," he responded with a large smile.

Mr. Holmes shifted uncomfortably on his horse, ready to leave post haste. I could see the discomfort in his body, how he poised himself on his horse. He was rigid and doing everything he could not to look back in Mr. Wickham's direction. With a curt nod towards myself, Mr. Holmes reared his horse and galloped away. Mr. Bingley startled at his friend's sudden departure.

"I do apologize, madams, sirs. We are on a tight schedule and must be off presently!"

Mr. Bingley was all manners and politeness, just as Jane was. Not only did they share a proclivity for manner, they also shared an authenticity to their politeness that was rare in civilized society. Most everyone shielded their true selves in their manners. They never meant the words that society required them to say. Jane and Mr. Bingley were a different sort. They meant all that they said. I viewed Jane's expression as she watched him ride off. Her subtlety hid her emotions well, as she rarely shared her true emotions, even shielding her true feelings from me, but I could see how honest the joy and affection she felt for Mr. Bingley was.

Mr. Wickham relaxed the moment Mr. Holmes left. The effect of his departure was instantaneous and palpable. Before their departure, the air had a near tangible feeling of tension, though none of my companions seemed to have noted the change.

As we continued on, our larger group divided into natural smaller ones. Lydia and Kitty ran jovially ahead of the group, discussing their ribbons and the excitement of the ball that Mr. Bingley had promised to throw. He had been so disappointed by how early the public ball ended that he said he would throw his own at Netherfield Park. Jane was engaged in conversation with Mr. Denny. I walked beside Mr. Wickham, grateful for the opportunity to ask him about the tension between himself and Mr. Holmes.

"Are you well acquainted with Mr. Holmes, sir?" I inquired.

Mr. Wickham looked at me quizzically, but as he saw my face, he must have realized how sure I was in my conviction that they had known each other at one point. I knew from their interaction that they had a past with one another and it was not a pleasant one.

"No, I never knew the man very well. He was hired on as a detective for a case that, frankly, ruined my life," he responded with more honesty than I had expected, especially as the details of his past with Mr. Holmes were certainly sordid and personal.

"I am sorry to hear that."

"And you, do you know him well?"

I shook my head in dissent. I felt slight guilt that I had brought up what was clearly a sore subject for the man. I did not know either man very well, as I had just met them both briefly and only quite recently.

"No, I met him briefly when I became acquainted with Mr. Bingley. I have not become well acquainted with him at all."

"Well, if I were you, I would consider myself lucky to not be acquainted with a man such as Mr. Holmes." Mr. Wickham was vehement in his disenchantment with the man.

"If you don't mind my prying, may I ask what the nature of your disagreement with the man is?" I carried the conversation on, surprised by the candid nature of Mr. Wickham's words. I found it difficult to tell if he spoke with such candor with just anyone, or if there was a significant ease to conversing with one another specifically.

"I grew up with no real father of my own. My true father was a man who took me under his wing and taught me to be a good man. He had another son, though, who was jealous of me. It only got worse after the man died and left a sizeable portion of his estate to me. I was slated to join the church, but his son took all that away from me. He accused me of something that I simply did not do and Mr. Holmes was the man he hired to, as they called it, prove I did so." He spoke matter-of-factly, as though he had accepted the sad truth that he was unable to do anything to change his past or prove that he had not done whatever was accused.

"I'm sorry that happened to you. It sounds like an awful ordeal." This was not sufficient in apologies for what horrible things poor Mr. Wickham had gone through, but I had no other words of comfort to offer the man.

"It happened a long time ago. I cannot help but be bitter about it, but I have done my best to move on from the injustice."

He certainly had bitterness left in him, as made evident by his hateful speech against Mr. Holmes. It was my feeling that Mr. Holmes had made many an enemy. Despite his dismissal of me at the ball I had warmed up to the gentleman as we discussed the complexities of observing human behavior. Focally I sympathized with Mr. Wickham and felt certain that whatever accusation made against him was sure to be false, however I did not believe that Mr. Holmes would wilfully give false evidence. It did not seem to be in his nature to deceive in such a manner.

I did not press Mr. Wickham further on the matter, as he was clearly not willing to give more detail than he already had. It was sure to be a minor infraction, as the man was not imprisoned in any capacity. Still, however minor the infraction, the repercussions were grand, clear as day. Mr. Wickham had lost all of his inheritance and could no longer pursue the life of the church.

It was not much farther that we were forced to part ways with the officers.

"It was a pleasure meeting you fine young ladies," Mr. Denny said, offering a small bow of the head in departure. "Unfortunately, this is where we must leave you, but we shall leave you in the capable hands of Mr. Collins."

He nodded towards Mr. Collins, who had stirred up enough courage to join Mr. Denny and Jane in their conversation. Mr. Collins responded with an over pronounced bow, sweeping his right foot forward in dramatic fashion.

"Shall we see you at the ball at Netherfield Park?" Lydia asked.

"I would not miss it," Mr. Denny responded.

He started to turn away, before stopping to wait for Mr. Wickham.

"Shall you go to the ball, too?" I asked, rather hopeful.

"Should you wish it, then I shall be there, Miss Bennet."

His reply made my cheeks flush. I was unused to attention such as that from men, though I did not mind it. He bowed politely and left with Mr. Denny.

I believe that must have been the last time I saw Mr. Wickham alive.

Our party made our way back to our home in Longbourn. Mr. Collins seemed to relax when the two officers departed. He did not enjoy their company. As far as I could see, he did not much enjoy the company of anyone but the sound of his own voice and possibly his patronage the Lady Catherine De Bourgh. He seemed to be a sham of a man, a conglomeration of quotes and sayings that were not used in real life, but were lines one could read from a page. All of his conversation was directly quoted from literature, and obviously practiced a multitude of times. There was nothing genuine about the man.

After a gruelling dinner and evening reading from Mr. Collins, Jane and I were thankful to leave for our room, where we could enjoy a reprieve from Mr. Collins' incessant chatter. The pair of us enjoyed our evenings together. Our room was where we shared the most intimate details of our souls, where we could be the most ourselves.

"Mr. Bingley is just what a gentleman should be," Jane said, a smile stretched across her face. "I am so pleased to have met him."

This kind of statement was as good as saying she loved him. Jane was so private with her feelings, I often found her to be a mystery, sure that she had more to say than she ever allowed herself to. I, on the other hand, could never hold my tongue, allowing my thoughts and emotions to run freely into the world. I did not have the talent that Jane possessed in hiding my emotions. By nature, I was less tactful than she.

"I am pleased for you, my dear, sweet Jane." I was overwhelmed by affection for my sister. "What are your thoughts on Mr. Wickham?" I asked.

I had continued to think about him long after we parted ways. I did not know how to think about the man, but I could not stop myself from thinking of him. He was handsome to be sure, one of the most handsome men I had ever laid eyes on, but I did not trust him. He seemed too charming to me, as though he had a secret that he had kept for a long time. It had to have something to do with what he had been accused of doing and that Mr. Holmes proved to be true.

"He seems like a perfectly agreeable man. Very handsome," she replied, teasing me.

I found him attractive, but there was more to him than met the eye. My thoughts were consumed by him and Mr. Holmes. I wanted desperately to know their history. Clearly, the case was something that Mr. Wickham wanted to hide. I did not blame him, as if I were accused of a crime, I am sure that I would want that information to remain private, but my very nature was to be curious about such things.

"Yes, he is. Very."

I could tell that Jane had been exhausted by the day. In truth, I found myself tired by the day's activities, as well. Mr. Collins had read to us for near an hour after dinner. His monotone voice, combined with the long walk to and from town, rendered us all overcome with sleepiness.

"He and Mr. Holmes know one another."

Jane had closed her eyes but had not yet fallen asleep. She did not inquire with words, but instead made a soft hmm sound in interest.

"Apparently Mr. Holmes helped in a false accusation against Mr. Wickham for some kind of crime or scandalous act."

Jane looked at me through one open eye. "That's quite a story. I'm sure that whatever the case, it was a misunderstanding of sort."

I laughed at her, always wanting to think the best of everyone.

"I bet he killed someone," I said to scandalize her.

It worked, as her eyes sprung open in shock. "Lizzy! How could you say such a horrible thing?"

I smiled at her. She gave me an exasperated expression before turning over and blowing out the candle that kept our room alight. This signified that she decided that it was time for the both of us to fall asleep. I could hear her soft snoring after just a moment of silence.

I, however, could not get to sleep so easily. My thoughts would not allow me to get any rest. I found my mind wandering over the events of the prior fortnight. Jane had met her match, so long as Mr. Collins did not extend a hand of marriage to her. I knew that if Mama caught wind of it, she would manipulate it so that it did not happen. She would want one of us to marry him, however. It would ensure the family's safety forever, and myself and my sisters would not have to worry about being turned out of our home after Papa died. Although this would be her desire, she would not have Jane marry him if she could help the situation. The advantageous marriage between Mr. Bingley and Jane was worth protecting, even if it meant that she would hazard offending Mr. Collins. I knew that should she be able to redirect his sights, they would then be set on me. I should not accept any proposal of marriage he would offer. This would be a selfish act on my part, but I could not abide by more than a few hours time with Mr. Collins, not to mention an entire lifetime with the man. It was my hope that Mama would offend Mr. Collins, not enough that he might turn us all out on the street, but enough that he would no longer wish to marry any of us or spend much time at Longbourn.

My mind continued to wander back to Mr. Wickham and Mr. Holmes. I knew that their past was important in someway. Both gentlemen had captured my attention for different reasons, but their hold on me was strong. I knew Mr. Wickham had also captured Lydia's attention. She had spent most of our walk in conversation with Mr. Denny, but even more of it staring at Mr. Wickham. There was a part of me that felt Mr. Wickham could not be trusted, and that part manifested itself not when he informed me of his sordid dealings with Mr. Holmes, but in the exchange of glances between he and Lydia.

# CHAPTER FOUR:
## Death at the Ball

"I will do your chores for you for a month, Lizzy, please!" Lydia begged, chasing me around the upper floor of the house. The house had been in an uproar with us all getting ready for the ball at Netherfield Park. Lydia had been asking me to lend her my best shoes for the ball.

"Lydia, you owe me months of chores already," I responded.

Lydia constantly offered up chores as payment for borrowing clothing items and the like. She never repaid them, although Jane and myself usually lent her things regardless. She wanted everything that we had, but that was the way of younger sisters, so we allowed her this one indulgence.

"I promise, Lizzy. Please, I need them for the ball."

"What if I need them for the ball?" Although I had no intention of not allowing Lydia to use my shoes, I could not give them up easily. Then she would be a nightmare. If she knew we gave our clothes up willingly, she would never stop requesting them of us. She batted her eyes at me dramatically. "Alright, fine. One month of chores, though, Lydia."

She jumped for joy and wrapped me in a hug before running off to get my shoes.

"She might do them this time. I believe she may want those shoes enough to actually do chores for them," Jane said, coming up behind me, watching our little sister bound down the hallway.

"I doubt it. Once she has them, she will not put another thought to doing the chores," I replied. Although the words sounded harsh, I did not mean them in such a way. I said them with a smile. I knew my younger sister well and loved her despite her quirks.

I had never seen Lydia and Kitty so excited. They could not wait for the ball. Mr. Bingley had announced it not long after our encounter on the way back from town. His sister had been the one to extend the invitation to us, which greatly upset our Mama. She felt it was a slight against Jane, as Mr. Bingley did not extend the invitation personally. Jane did not feel offended. She was thankful that Caroline, Mr. Bingley's sister, was extending her welcome. It felt as though the invitation coming from her was some kind of precursor to inviting her to join the family. Of course, the way Jane and I felt may have been our own hopes skewing our interpretation of the act.

It had been a long while since there was something so extravagant to look forward to in town. Jane had let her guard down for the first time in a while. She was so happy to see Mr. Bingley. From my perspective, it appeared as though the ball was a lavish excuse for Mr. Bingley and Jane to see one another. Of course, I did not know Mr. Bingley's mind, but it felt like this would be the case on his side of the matter, as well.

The only unenthusiastic member of the Bennet family was, of course, Mary. She had no interest in balls and had come near to refusing to go, though she knew as well as I that attendance at the Bingley ball would be compulsory. My only hope for Mary at the ball was that she would not try to take up the piano and entertain the guests. She had talent playing the piano forte, but had very little talent in singing. She often took up the piano forte in an attempt to entertain. Typically, people were kind and allowed her to play without the humiliation of discovering that her talent was not so great. I feared that the guests at Mr. Bingley's ball would not be so kind. Papa had already urged Mary to avoid the piano forte, his fears being similar to my own.

Even Papa had become excited to go to the ball, and it was a break in his usual character. His comfort was books and his study. He did not much like being sociable, so it surprised me that he seemed as though he could not wait to go to the ball. I thought it might be his excitement for Jane to be with Mr. Bingley, but I could not be sure of his reasons.

When we arrived, we were greeted warmly by our hosts. Netherfield Park was magnificent on its own, but decorated for a ball, it seemed to me to be an unreal sight. The gentlemen and ladies studded the estate with their beauty. I myself could not be swayed by beauty alone, but I could not deny that my breath had been taken away by the sight. Mr. Bingley could hardly stop himself from speaking with Jane longer than would be appropriate as we entered. Caroline, Mr. Bingley's sister, stopped him from paying too close attention to Jane and continued on in the line of welcoming us into their home. She was a shrewd woman, who certainly understood that her brother had budding feelings for Jane. When I saw her usher Jane through, interrupting her brother's prolonged greeting, I began to suspect that she was not as supportive of the match as I had desired her to be.

Mr. Collins continued to bring embarrassment to us. He discovered that Mr. Holmes would be in attendance and had begun his search. In fact, he was in search of any name that had status in attendance. Mr. Collins seemed to be the type to find status in his acquaintances, and searched for more at every chance. The true reason for his desire to meet Mr. Holmes was that he was well acquainted with the nephew of Miss Catherine De Burgh. His appreciation for the woman extended beyond just herself and her family members, to their acquaintances as well. I was engaged in conversation with Mama, Jane, and Caroline when I noticed that Mr. Holmes stood nearby to us, conversing with a group of people, and that Mr. Collins was closing in on the man. I turned my focus away from the conversation at hand and listened in on Mr. Collins' attempt at introducing himself to Mr. Holmes.

"Hello, Mr. Holmes. It is an honor to make your acquaintance," Mr. Collins said with a stiff bow towards Mr. Holmes, who jumped at the intrusion and looked down upon the squirrelly man.

"Yes," he said curtly, returning the bow. "And you are?"

"Mr. Collins, sir."

Mr. Holmes nodded again at the man before turning away. It was then that Mr. Collins coughed to capture his attention once again. Mr. Holmes turned to face him, clearly finding the man as much of an annoyance as I did.

"Sorry, did you need assistance?"

"No, of course not," he stammered. "I know about your work as a consulting detective."

"Do you need detecting?"

"No, you misunderstand me, sir. My patroness is the Lady Catherine De Burgh. You worked on a case for her nephew not long ago. Mr. Darcy was the name."

Mr. Holmes looked at the man as though he had started to speak a foreign language in the middle of their conversation. I had to stifle a laugh as I digested Mr. Holmes' expression.

"Pleasure to make your acquaintance," Mr. Holmes responded, giving the man another bow, quite obviously feigning respect for Mr. Collins before once again turning away from him and returning to his conversation.

Mr. Collins tried once again to catch his attention, but Mr. Holmes simply pretended to ignore the man's coughs. I had no doubt that Mr. Holmes recalled the exact case that Mr. Collins was bringing up. I could make the safe assumption that his memory was extensive and clear. He seemed far too clever to me to be unable to recall any fact he might need to. When Mr. Holmes turned to face his group, the man met my eye shortly. Though he did not smile, I could sense a mischievous glint in his eyes.

It was not long before he made his way over to Mama, Caroline, Jane, and I along with Mr. Bingley. Mama was overjoyed with Mr. Bingley's appearance. She had been waiting with impatience for him to arrive and ask Jane for a dance. She still felt disillusioned with Mr. Holmes, not wanting to forgive him for his poor social manners.

Mr. Bingley invited Jane to join him for the next dance. Should a person be able to die of happiness, I believe that she could have. Caroline gave another brief but clear indicator that she did not approve of the match. It was not in her words, but her expression. I could see a subtle change in her manner as Mr. Bingley requested that Jane join him on the dance floor. Her face fell slightly and I could imagine her manner of disapproval. We were not so well off as they. It would clearly be an advantageous marriage for Jane. Caroline might not believe that Jane's feelings were genuine, or she simply believed us to be of a lower station than would be proper to marry her brother.

"Miss Bennet, would you do me the honor?" Mr. Holmes asked.

I startled at the request. "I'm sorry?" I asked, although I heard and understood his original question.

"Do me the honor of dancing the next dance with me?"

"It would be my pleasure," I responded immediately.

Mama and Caroline looked equally upset by the request and my subsequent acceptance, though I knew their reasons were different. Mama simply did not like Mr. Holmes, but Caroline was more than just acquainted with him and seemed to enjoy his company. I believed that she felt slighted by being overlooked by Mr. Holmes, especially as she was the only single woman he danced with at the previous ball. I did not think that she had feelings for the man, but rather she felt slighted when any man did not express a preference for her.

Mr. Holmes and I joined each other in the next dance. Dances were interesting, as they were the only time that young men and women were allowed to be engaged in conversation without some kind of chaperone. Although conversations could still be overheard, there was a degree of freedom that was not afforded at any other time. It was because of this that Mr. Holmes asked me to join him in a dance. Never did we share romantic feelings or consider the other in such a manner. Though we became less concerned with public appearances as time went on, oftentimes when the case called for it, we would join one another on the dance floor to have discussions without drawing attention to ourselves. This was the first dance of that nature.

"Miss Bennet, I do believe you have been paying more attention as of late."

"If by paying attention you mean observing, then yes, I have, Mr. Holmes."

"Do you think that you are talented at it?"

I had not considered this question and was caught off guard by it. I did not understand how one was to know if they had talent at observation, as it appeared to be all conjecture unless somehow your observations manifested themselves in physical evidence. A personal observation could not be something one had talent for. Although, it was with this skill Mr. Holmes became a detective.

"I do not know if I understand your query."

"Your deductions from observation, are they accurate? Do you have talent?"

"I am not sure if I am yet able to gauge how accurate my assumptions are."

Mr. Holmes let out a laugh. "Very diplomatic answer, Miss Bennet." He paused briefly as the dance moved us away from one another. "But," he continued, "what you are doing is not making assumptions, but making accurate deductions based on what it is you are observing with your eyes. There are not and should be no assumptions made. True talent in deduction is knowing that."

"Then I suppose I have not been observing and deducting for a long enough period of time to say that I have talent at it. All my observations have only led to conjecture for myself."

"And what conjectures have you made thus far?" The man was quizzing me. Seeing if I had talent in what he was an artist in. I did not know how to react or why he had taken such an interest in my observational skills. For that matter, I had no inkling as to why I had even begun to make such astute observations of those around me. His power of suggestion at the public ball had been enough to make me want to try out deduction and observing for myself. Not that I had never practiced observation before. I was by nature an observer of those around me, but never before had I thought about the conclusions that one could draw based on observation alone. Mr. Holmes would not drop his line of questioning, which began to frustrate me.

"You and Mr. Wickham have an interesting past," I said. "You worked on a case that made him lose everything. He has implied that your deduction was untrue, that you feigned evidence to make him appear guilty of what he did not commit."

"Mr. Wickham never fails to convey how ill I treated him, in his own version of events." The mention of the name did not seem to upset him in the same way the mention of his name upset Mr. Wickham.

"What is your opinion?" he asked. The mention of the man had not bothered him, but the accusation of falsifying evidence did. "That I would do such a thing as feign my testimony to make Mr. Wickham appear guilty?"

There was an anger that I had not thought him capable of behind the words. His profession was his dearest possession in life. I had not seen him show the same level of respect to anything else. Although he appeared more put together than he had at the public ball, his appearance was still disheveled at best, which made him stick out in the current company.

"I do no believe you would." I had made up my mind in this matter. That Mr. Wickham had secrets. To be sure, Mr. Holmes had them as well, but Mr. Wickham not only possessed secrets, but lies. From my perspective, it seemed as though Mr. Wickham was guilty of whatever he had been accused of and simply maintained his innocence in a ploy to garner pity. To avoid taking responsibility for his actions, he blamed Mr. Holmes for what he called false testimony. Mr. Holmes relaxed after I stated this belief. "I think your alliance to the truth and your respect for your position, consulting detective, is far too great for you to be swayed to give false evidence."

"If I did not have my good reputation in solving cases and gathering evidence, then I would have nothing."

Something in the way he spoke expressed to me the truth of how little he would have should he lose his position. A wave of pity for the man washed over me momentarily. He most certainly had only a few people in the world to rely upon.

"I believe that to be true," I responded.

The dance came upon its end, but before it came to a halt, Mr. Holmes lent me a warning: "Guard yourself and your sisters against Mr. Wickham. He is charming, but dangerous news for young ladies of good standing. I have seen how young Lydia looks upon the man, and you must warn her against him. The consequences of the contrary would be detrimental to her and to your family."

With that, he left my side, disappearing into the crowd. Strange, his talent to disappear despite his odd appearance. His warning had left a knot in the pit of my stomach. I surveyed the crowd in the dance hall, looking for Lydia and Mr. Wickham. I had forgotten that Mr. Wickham should be in attendance. The nature of Mr. Holmes' warning made my mind run wild with the possibilities of what Mr. Wickham had done in the past to an unsuspecting young lady of good standing. Lydia was sure to be the most unsuspecting lady I had ever come across and her silliness knew no bounds. She was drawn to Mr. Wickham and I had suspicions that he knew how to take advantage of that. Mr. Holmes had disappeared and I could not locate Mr. Wickham or Lydia. I felt in my heart that something was not right.

"Charlotte, have you seen Lydia this evening?" I asked, joining my dear friend at the outskirts of the room. Charlotte was a dear and had been entertaining Mr. Collins for the better part of the evening. She was now standing alone at the edge of the room, attempting to keep her distance from the man to enjoy a break.

"I have not seen her. I am sorry Lizzy. Is something the matter? You appear rather agitated."

I had become rather distraught from not being able to locate either Mr. Wickham or Lydia. I feared that he was manipulating her into doing things she would otherwise not. Lydia was but fifteen years old and susceptible to the suggestion of men. No matter how foolish, should she believe him to be in love with her, she would go with him.

"I have learned some troubling news about Mr. Wickham, the officer I told you about not long ago. I fear that the two are together."

Charlotte immediately took my concern seriously, her hand raising to her mouth. "I shall help you locate them."

We did not need to search for long before we heard the screams. As I raced in the direction they came from, I could feel in my very soul that the screams were being ripped from Lydia's lungs. The entire ball had taken pause at her shouts, the music stopping abruptly as the screams echoed throughout Netherfield Park.

When I arrived on the scene, I was relieved that Lydia appeared to be alright. They were in a room far from the rest of the gathering. It had not been designed to be a part of the ball that evening and as such was dark, the only light coming from the rooms surrounding it. Mr. Holmes had arrived on the scene prior to myself. He was holding Lydia as she shouted and screamed. My view was obscured by the dark, but I could just make out Mr. Wickham lying on the ground. My thoughts raced to put the pieces of the puzzle together.

It was not until Mr. Bingley came up behind me with a candle that I saw the full scene. Mr. Wickham was lying dead on the ground. He did not appear to be bloody; the cause of death was not apparent. However, there was blood on the wall, the letters "RACHE" written in it. The scene was grisly to be sure. I had never seen such a thing in my life.

As soon as Lydia calmed enough to notice me there, she ran into my arms sobbing.

"He's dead, Lizzy. Mr. Wickham is dead." She repeated the statement over and over again with no pause. The event had traumatized her, as it would most. I myself had a morbid curiosity and wanted to uncover the truth behind his mysterious death.

"This is now a murder scene and investigation. No one may come or go," Mr. Holmes said with authority.

Mr. Bingley nodded, his face pale. As more people came to see the cause of the screams, chaos and commotion began to break out. Women fainted and cried out, men became angry and suspicious. They also wanted to leave, stating they clearly had no part in the death and as such they should be allowed to leave of their own free will.

Mr. Bingley was shaken, but managed to convince near everyone to stay until they could get some answers. Immediately, someone went to notify the police, though we were not equipped for such a crime. It would have to be Mr. Holmes who ran the investigation, at least until the proper authorities could arrive.

"Miss Bennet," Mr. Holmes said to gain my attention, which had been focused on Lydia entirely.

"Yes?" I asked, trying to hold Lydia up. She was conscious, but seemed not to have the ability to keep herself standing.

"I will be requiring your assistance with this case," he answered.

And with that statement, in that moment, my life was forever changed.

# CHAPTER FIVE:
## An Indecent Proposal

Mama and Papa were so concerned with Lydia that they took no notice of me joining in the investigation. Mr. Holmes managed to keep everyone from coming into the room where Mr. Wickham lay dead.

"How can you be sure that he was murdered?" I asked, standing a distance from the body.

He motioned to the word written in blood on the wall.

"There is no blood on Mr. Wickham. Maybe the two incidences are not connected?" I had never seen death before, but I had to imagine that it was not common that a man as young and healthy as Mr. Wickham would be killed without a bloody fight.

"I do not believe in coincidences in the most likely of scenarios. In a situation such as this, they must be related, however odd the circumstances."

I turned my attention from the lifeless body on the ground to the bloody word on the wall. I wondered what it could mean. It was nothing like I had seen before. I was familiar with the German word "rache," meaning revenge, and did not have any illusions about the probability that there were many a man and woman that wanted to exact revenge on the man.

"What do you think it means?"

"I think it's a message," he said in an offhand manner.

"What do you mean, a message?" I queried. It felt as though he was disregarding the significance of the letters entirely. "Could it be the killer trying to tell us something? Rache means revenge in German; perhaps that is the motive here."

Mr. Holmes looked at me with a dry expression of boredom. I got the impression that this was the exact conclusion he had come to, as well.

"The idea of leaving behind this message to tell us why he committed a murder is ludicrous, but I am certain the man meant it as a message telling us the true crime was whatever Mr. Wickham did to the gentleman who committed the murder and the real reason behind the murder of our Mr. Wickham."

"And what do you suggest that is?"

"I have no idea." The man was crouched over the body with a magnifying glass that appeared to have been in his coat pocket the entire time. He lifted Mr. Wickham's hand up, examining it, and placed it back to the ground. In truth, Mr. Holmes appeared to be more comfortable dealing with a corpse than he was dealing with living, breathing people. He was at ease in the crime scene, and I had a front row seat to view how he examined and came to conclusions based on those examinations. I could almost compare it to watching da Vinci with a canvas and a brush, watching Mr. Holmes with a corpse and nothing but a few clues. "This man is sure to have been poisoned."

"Have you deduced this because of the lack of blood or bodily injury?"

"Yes. He also has white residue on the tips of his fingers from a pill of some type. It is my belief that this man ingested a pill that caused his demise."

I could not fathom what would make a man as fit and strong as Mr. Wickham seemingly willingly take a pill that caused his death. I assumed it was willingly as there was no sign of a struggle in the room. If the murder had taken place elsewhere and the body moved, his killer would have to be almost inhumanly strong to move such a man from a different location.

"Do you think he took the pill of his own volition?"

"I would think it so. The residue from the pill is on his own fingers as though he took the pill himself. We shall need to make queries in order to discover who has committed this crime." I had assumed as such would be the case. No investigation was complete without interrogations. It seemed that no matter what evidence could be gathered from the body, the way to find the guilty party was through speaking with the people who witnessed it. Mr. Holmes' tone changed as he looked at me. "I will need to speak with Lydia."

"I know we must, but she will need time to calm herself before we can speak to her." I knew that Lydia would be a key witness to the murder. More than likely, she was the last person to see Mr. Wickham alive, and based on how shaken poor Lydia was, she may have even seen his death. I could still hear Lydia wailing in the distance, where most of the guests had returned to the main hall.

Mr. Bingley had decided that he would send some people home. There were far too many people in attendance to keep them for long. He was preoccupied with ensuring that my family was doing alright, as they were all shaken for Lydia.

Mr. Holmes and I had been observing the crime scene for a while now. He was silent for most of it and I simply stood there watching him make his observations. I guess silent was not the right word for it. He spent most of his time muttering to himself. Were I not already acquainted with the man, I surely would think him to have some kind of insanity. To be frank, though I did know him, I remained unconvinced that he did not have any insanity.

"I think you should be the one to question her, Miss Bennet."

"You want me to interview her?" I had never conducted an interview before and did not know that I could or why Mr. Holmes would want me to. I had not put much thought into why Mr. Holmes had me assisting him at all. It was odd for him to request a woman to assist him in the first place, let alone me, a woman with whom he was barely acquainted. I never asked him that question, the why of it all. I did not much care to. I found myself too wrapped up in the excitement of the case and the intrigue of Mr. Holmes.

"You have a connection to her. She will more willingly speak with you than she would with me."

His response made sense. Lydia would certainly be sure to answer any questions I might ask. I did not want to put her through that, though. She was a fragile girl, and I knew that she would not be able to face what she saw for a second time.

"I cannot rightly ask her questions about what she witnessed tonight yet. She will need time to recover, Mr. Holmes."

"No, we can't wait. She needs to be questioned immediately or she will forget the details that she saw."

I did not disagree with his assessment of the situation, but I still could not question my sister in her state in good conscience. "Let us gather all that we can from here and then go to her for questions."

Mr. Holmes nodded in agreement. "I have gathered most of what is possible from the body and the room." This startled me, as I did not even know what to make of the scene we were looking at. Mr. Holmes grinned at me, as though he enjoyed my ineptitude. "Mr. Wickham took poison that killed him, and he took the pill of his own volition, but he was murdered. There is no blood on the body, but there is the writing on the wall in blood. Given that, the blood must belong to the murderer.

"The murderer would have been someone who held a grudge against the man, but given who Mr. Wickham was in life, he had no shortage of men and women who had a grudge against him.

The murderer was a man, six feet tall, though his feet are disproportionate to his height. He was wearing a square-toed shoe and he smoked a cigar."

"How do you know all that?" I was shocked by how detailed his deductions were. These were not simple observations and assumptions. He pulled distinct and (he seemed sure) accurate facts from the things he observed. Mr. Holmes appeared to be having the best time of his life telling me all that he was able to deduce from his looking around the room.

"Nothing more than simple deduction, Miss Bennet. Shall we question your sister now?" He asked the question with more sensitivity than I expected from the man. He showed little compassion normally, but here he was gentle in his delivery. He knew that I would not stand for an abrasive attack on Lydia. Asking her questions forcefully was not something that I would allow to happen. "We will only ask her what she can handle," he reassured.

"I suppose it is time. She must have calmed down enough. I do not hear her cries any longer. If she is resting, can we allow her to sleep?"

He nodded in agreement.

"Thank you." I was appreciative of this allowance. Should she not be related to me I doubted he would allow such niceties.

As we were leaving, the doctor showed up to take away Mr. Wickham's body.

Mr. Holmes stayed with the doctor, ensuring that nothing aside from the body was disturbed in the crime scene. It would be a few days before officials from Scotland Yard could arrive at Netherfield Park.

I discovered my family huddled together in the drawing room. Mr. Bingley had taken them away from the rest of the crowd in order to give Lydia privacy. He tried offering her a room, but she did not want to be away from everyone. Lydia was still weeping, laying on Mama's lap. Her eyes were closed, though, so I could not be sure if she was sleeping or not. Jane came up to me as I entered the room.

"Lizzy, where have you been?" she asked me in a hushed tone.

"Mr. Holmes wanted me to assist him." She gave me a quizzical look, but I continued before she could ask more questions. "I need to speak with Lydia. Is she doing alright?"

Jane was immediately consumed by concern for our younger sister. Kitty had fallen asleep with her arms wrapped around Lydia. I could see now that Lydia had not fallen asleep. Her eyes were open and they were red with tears and exhaustion as one would expect from anyone who had gone through such an ordeal. Papa was pacing around the room and Mary had clearly fallen asleep a while before, as she was asleep in an arm chair.

"I do not think that she will ever be the same again," Jane whispered, looking back at Lydia with pity.

"Do you think that she will be okay with me asking her about what she may have seen?"

Jane shook her head. "Lizzy, you cannot be considering asking her to relive what she has just seen?"

She was horrified by my query and I could not help but feel an overwhelming sense of guilt for having even considered such a thing. Jane had not asked to make me feel guilt, but that was the result. I could not imagine what the horror of seeing Mr. Wickham's death had done to Lydia.

"Mr. Holmes needs to know what she saw or did not see in order to find out who killed Mr. Wickham."

Papa heard me speaking to Jane although we were whispering our words. "Lizzy, that is not going to happen. Lydia is in no condition to speak, let alone answer questions that she does not have answers for." Papa's voice was stern. He was angry with me for the suggestion.

I was angry with him for impeding the investigation. I had made no indication that my queries would be unanswerable. My plan was quite the opposite. I wanted only to ask her questions she would be able to answer. I readied my reply, but before I could speak, Lydia did.

"What do you need to know, Lizzy?" She sniffled, raising herself from Mama's lap. Kitty did not wake, but moved her own head to Mama's lap and made herself comfortable. Mama was surely horrified by the death of Mr. Wickham, but her maternal instincts had kept her nerves at bay. It was surprising to see how well Mama and her nerves were handling all the excitement. She had started to stroke Kitty's hair as soon as Lydia rose from her seat. "If I can help, Lizzy. Ask me what you need to."

"Are you certain?" I asked Lydia.

She nodded at me. She appeared to be weak, as though it was hard for her to even stand, but she did it. I felt another wave of guilt come over me, although this time it was not because I needed to ask her questions, but because I had believed her to be so fragile that she could not handle it.

"Can you just go through your evening with me, Lydia? Tell me what happened."

"I had been asked to dance by a gentleman, I do not remember who, but before the dance began, Mr. Wickham came up to me." She brought her hand to her face, wiping away a tear. "He said that he could not stop thinking of me from the moment we met. He said many things, to woo me, I suppose, but he suggested we speak privately and I agreed. What a fool I am." She let an angry huff out, as though she were mad at herself for what happened. “When we went to the room, he forced himself on me.”

She looked at Papa nervously as she said this. He stopped pacing and his hand went to his mouth in shock and upset, but he said nothing, allowing Lydia to finish her tale. “I ran away to the adjoining room. I was so fearful. He did not follow me, though. I stayed in the other room just shy of an hour, trying to remain hidden. It was then that I heard the thump of him falling. I ran to the room to find him lying there on the ground.” It was here in her story that she began sobbing. “I’m sorry,” she whispered. She continued to repeat the phrase through her tears as she ran back over to Mama, who opened her arms to her.

My heart broke for Lydia. She had always had an innocence to her that she would never have again. Mr. Wickham had taken that from her even before he had died and before she had seen his lifeless body. A young woman should not have to apologize for a man taking advantage of her. She had been sobbing not just because she had stumbled upon Mr. Wickham’s body, but also because of the shame she felt for leaving with him in the first place.

“Thank you, Lydia. You’ve helped tremendously,” I said, kneeling in front of Lydia and stroking her hair. “Thank you.”

"He scared me and was a scoundrel to be sure, but that doesn't mean he should be dead," she cried and turned her face into Mama.

Mr. Bingley arrived with an offer for us to stay the night as I made my exit. In the meantime, all the other guests had taken their leave. Once the physician was able to take away Mr. Wickham's corpse, Mr. Holmes had told Mr. Bingley to allow everyone in attendance to leave. He seemed certain that he would be able to find the killer whether the restless group stayed at Netherfield Park or not.

It was not until later that I discovered the real reason Mr. Holmes had allowed all the attendants of the ball to take their leave. He knew that none of them had committed the murder, that the responsible party would be staying—that it must be someone from my own party or Mr. Bingley's.

# CHAPTER SIX:

## A Small Clue

The next morning, we awoke at Netherfield Park. The lot of us had slept late, as no one wanted to wake and deal with the weight of Mr. Wickham's death. Mr. Bingley was already speaking of leaving Netherfield Park, as he could not bear to stay in a house where such a ghastly thing occurred. Were it anyone else, this kind of speech would render me weary and suspicious, but I knew that Mr. Bingley simply did not have it in his character to commit such a terrible crime.

Mr. Collins had fled back to his homestead as soon as the body had been discovered. He did not want to be a part of something so amoral. I am sure that he would prefer that word of his association with such a heinous act not get back to his patroness. I hoped any dream or wish of marrying either me or one of my sisters had been expunged from his mind with his departure.

Currently, however, I had more pressing matters occupying my thoughts. I had been reeling over Mr. Holmes' description of the assailant. Six feet tall. Small feet. Square-toed shoes. Cigar smoker.

I could not place a man of that description at the ball the previous evening. I continued to go over each man I laid eyes on, but none of them matched this likeness. It was an odd descriptor, but it was within the realm of both possibility and probability. A man would have to be larger than Mr. Wickham to have overpowered him in order to get him to take the pill that killed him. The square-toed shoes were obvious, as was the cigar. Through observing the crime scene, if one looked closely enough, there were footprints on the floors matching a square toed boot and there were ashes that could only have come from a cigar. I did not know how Mr. Holmes came to the conclusion that his feet were disproportionate to his body, though my assumption was that the footprints combined with the fact that Mr. Wickham had to have been killed by someone larger than himself allowed him to deduce the height and size of his feet, and the fact that they were not proportionate.

Lydia was still resting when we broke our fast in the morning. She had been through an ordeal and needed her rest more than any of us. It was here that Mr. Bingley broke the news he would be moving as soon as this business was dealt with.

"I shall be leaving Netherfield Park once we bring the man who committed this act to justice. I cannot in good conscience remain here, under this roof, knowing what has taken place."

"Rightly so, I could not abide by it, dear brother," Caroline Bingley replied.

By all appearances, Miss Bingley seemed to be less shaken than the rest of us about the murder. Mr. Holmes had clearly not gotten a wink of sleep, which made me feel guilty for getting hours of good rest. I had been exhausted by the previous day and despite the horrifying events, I was able to sleep soundly and for many hours. I knew it was not the violence of the events that kept Mr. Holmes awake, however. He was consumed by the case, running it over in his mind, trying to discover who the killer was from simple observations and Lydia's detailing of the events.

"I understand why you must go, but we shall all mourn you after you depart," Jane said softly.

The candidness of her statement took us all aback. It was very forward of her to say such a thing. Mr. Bingley turned to look at Jane and agreed that he would mourn their parting as well. The death of Mr. Wickham seemed to give them the ability to speak their minds in a way they were fearful to do before. Miss Bingley looked aghast at their confessions, but remained quiet. Mama, though she was still consumed with worry for Lydia, near burst into tears at Jane's and Mr. Bingley's statements. Whether they were tears of happiness that the two had finally made their feelings for one another clear or with sadness that Mr. Bingley should be leaving shortly, I do not know.

"When shall you depart?" Papa asked sullenly.

"I would not feel right to depart until after the case is solved, so that should depend on Mr. Holmes."

Mr. Holmes calmly answered, "I shall have the truth discovered in just a short while. I am close to cracking it now."

I peered at Mr. Holmes over the top of my glass, unsure whether he was fibbing to put everyone at ease or if he truly believed he would be able to solve the case within a short time.

It was unorthodox, but Mr. Bingley extended our welcome until Lydia seemed to be strong enough to leave with us. She had been shaken by the events more than we originally thought and had been unable to get out of her bed since her head hit the pillow the night before. It was as though Mr. Bingley felt responsible because Mr. Wickham was killed under his roof, though I knew him to be innocent of any direct relation with the crime.

As we left breakfast, I went to confront Mr. Holmes. He knew more about Mr. Wickham than the rest of us and I needed to know what it was he knew about the man. I also needed to know if he had been bluffing about being close to solving the case in order to quell anxieties.

"Mr. Holmes, are you really close to figuring out who the murderer was?"

"Oh, I already know."

"You could not possibly know already."

He smiled at me, that same mischievous glimmer in his eyes and I knew that what he said was the truth.

"Then why have you not apprehended the man yet?" I said. Although I had not been in the world of crime solving for long, I was quite certain that the apprehension of the culprit was an important part of the process.

"Well, Miss Bennet, I have not apprehended him yet, because the true killer was not a man."

I balked at this. Both sexes were, of course, capable of violence, but it would be rather unheard of for a woman to kill a man in cold blood. I was also sure that I would recall if I had seen a woman of six feet at the ball.

"How is that possible? By your own description of the assailant, it can't possibly be a woman."

Mr. Holmes nodded. "Well, yes."

"So your description was inaccurate?"

He scoffed at the very notion. "No. Not in the slightest."

Mr. Holmes had lost me. I was sure he had gone insane at some point during the night as there was no way his description could be accurate and the assailant could be a woman. The two negated one another, yet he was insisting both to be true.

He gazed at my puzzled expression for a moment before launching into his explanation. "Well, it was a man and a woman to be more accurate. A woman paid our six-foot-tall attacker to kill Mr. Wickham. This was a hired hit. And the woman who hired him is still under this roof. She will lead us to her hired man."

"A woman under this roof committed this murder?" I asked, a dreadful feeling in my stomach rising up. "Even though she is a woman, why have you not taken her into custody?"

"Because I cannot yet prove motive."

"What more motive do you require? We have revenge in blood on the wall and by Lydia's account of Mr. Wickham's behavior towards her, it is not difficult to see what a woman might want revenge against the wicked man for."

"I believe that RACHE was a diversion, something the murderer wrote on the wall to keep us distracted and keep our focus away from the true murderer, which would be the woman who paid to have Mr. Wickham killed."

"You clearly believe you know who it is. Will you tell me, sir?"

I had my own suspicions based off of his theory. No one in my family could possibly be a suspect. None of us had known Mr. Wickham long enough to have enough rage against him to do such a thing, nor did we possess the funds and the means to hire a killer. That left only Mr. Bingley's sisters.

"I discovered a ring on the floor underneath the body, as though it were a calling card of some kind. It told me who must be the killer."

He again ignored my request to know which woman hired the assailant. He was a theatrical man and would not reveal his climax before it was time.

"The ring is petite. It is not a wedding band, but rather a piece of jewelry meant to accessorize, to flaunt, which tells me that the offending woman was fairly well off. You and your family are clearly not suspects." He meant this in a reassuring manner, but I could not help but take some offense at the statement. "Which leaves only the Bingley sisters. I have known them both well for a while now, and I believe them both to be capable of something like this. I have yet to discover what either of them should gain from Mr. Wickham's death." He was clearly upset that he could not figure out this piece of the puzzle for himself.

Rather than continuing on this subject, I stated, "I would like to know about what happened between yourself and Mr. Wickham in the past." This had been biting at me for a long while now and though I did not think it relevant to solving the case, I was not requesting that he speak to the nature of their relationship, I was telling him to.

"It has no pertinence to this case, but I shall tell you regardless. I do not believe you have given me a choice in the matter. I was hired to find Mr. Wickham by a wealthy gentleman. Mr. Wickham had taken his younger sister, Georgiana Darcy, a girl of but fifteen, just like your Lydia, with the promise to wed her. He doubled back on his promise as soon as he discovered that he would not be able to touch her rather large inheritance, leaving the girl heartbroken. The man hired me to find Mr. Wickham so that he would remain quiet about the situation, saving the poor girl's reputation. It was different from my normal sort of work, but I took the job anyway.

"The really terrible part is that the gentleman who hired me, his father practically raised Mr. Wickham as his own and left him some money after he died. Mr. Wickham lost it all to gambling, women, and libation. It was only when this ran out that he returned and manipulated the young girl into running away with him. Although he denied it, and apparently does still to this day, he accepted the hush money without question and I had not seen him since, until the other day on the way to town. That was how I met Mr. Bingley, actually. He is the closest companion of the gentleman who hired me. He aided me in the search for Mr. Wickham."

My mind raced following the story and suddenly, I had an idea. "Were either of Mr. Bingley's sisters involved in the search, or at the very least knew what was happening?"

"Neither were a part of the search, but I believe that both knew the story. Miss Bingley cared for the young girl once we got her back. She did not leave her side for many days. The girl was shaken and heartbroken, worried about her reputation and shaming the family. She was much like Lydia in many ways, both take hardship similarly in the inability to rise from bed or stop weeping."

"That is your motive, sir," I said without hesitation. I knew that should Mr. Wickham have left Lydia in this same state and not have been dead, I would have wanted to hire someone to kill him, as well. It was a ghastly thing to think, and I would not have admitted it out loud, but it was the truth. I felt a fierce protectiveness over Lydia and all my other sisters. Should someone hurt them, I would want to hurt the one who brought them pain.

"What is?" he asked, looking genuinely perplexed. It seemed as though the man had no concept of the relationships people share and how those can motivate even the kindest souls to do the darkest deeds.

"Miss Bingley wanted Mr. Wickham to pay for what he did to the young girl she cared about. She was tormented by the pain he caused and could not abide by it any longer. She did it out of love for the girl and hatred of Mr. Wickham."

Mr. Holmes lit up at my deduction. He may be good with observations of clues and inanimate objects, but my skill seemed to lie in the observation and understanding of human nature.

"You are not incorrect, Miss Bennet," Miss Bingley said coolly, making me jump.

Mr. Holmes' smile faltered as she stepped forward from the shadows of the doorway in which she'd been lurking. I did not know how much she had heard of our conversation, but surely it was enough.

"But that was not my only reasoning for hiring a man to kill Mr. Wickham." She spoke calmly and softly, as though she knew she would eventually be discovered before she had even committed the act.

"What was your other motivation?" Mr. Holmes asked.

I could feel my heartbeat through my whole body and my blood rush in my veins.

He added, "And why leave the ring?"

Mr. Holmes' curiosity was as palpable as my own. There was not a question that could be asked that we were uninterested in hearing the answer to.

"The ring was not purposeful. The plan was to get Mr. Wickham alone and distract him, but he had plans of his own. When I saw him steal away with Lydia, it only solidified my resolve to see him dead. I seduced Mr. Wickham after I heard Lydia run out crying. It was not hard, as the man will accept any partner, willing or otherwise. I would not let him do to another girl what he did to Georgiana. I suppose at some point, he pulled the ring from my finger, though I did not notice it. Add pickpocket to the list of crimes Mr. Wickham committed without answering to.

"I hired a man named Mr. Hope to kill him. While I distracted Mr. Wickham, Mr. Hope crept into the room and made sure he was cornered. He had no trouble with this, as Mr. Wickham was intimidated by a man larger than himself. Mr. Hope has a specific methodology that I could not make him sway from. The man, I assume to quell his own religious guilt, gives his victims a choice between two pills. One pill is harmless. The other contains a poison that will render the victim unconscious in seconds and dead within minutes. Mr. Hope said that whichever pill was chosen would then be the will of God. Mr. Wickham chose the poisoned pill, so evidently, it was the will of God that he is dead."

She ended her speech in a tone of vindictive spite that was almost tangible and harsh enough that I would believe it capable of slicing through steel.

"You have not given your other reason, sister," Mr. Bingley said, making the three of us jump.

As we turned, we discovered that not just he, but Papa and Jane had heard the entirety of Miss Bingley's hateful speech. Mr. Bingley had tears welling in his eyes, unable to stop them from pouring over.

"Charles," Miss Bingley gasped. In contrast to her harsh tone, her brother's name came out as a mere whisper, barely a breath.

"What was your other motivation?" Mr. Bingley demanded, raising his voice for what I imagine to be the first time in his life.

"Her." Miss Bingley pointed towards Jane. "I could not have you marrying so below your rank. I knew that should something like Mr. Wickham's death occur here and in such a public manner, you would no longer want to stay. It is not just their status that is so far below us, dear brother, but her family has shown such impropriety over our time in knowing them. I know it to be an advantageous match, and Mrs. Bennet has been speaking of your non-existent engagement for weeks now. I should not think that Miss Bennet's feelings for you are genuine." Miss Bingley lost her vehemence in this speech. The fear of repercussions guided her now, and she shied away from her brother's sharp gaze.

"My feelings are more genuine than you would ever know." To my surprise, it was Jane who responded to Miss Bingley's accusation. She had an anger in her that I had not seen before. "I care for your brother more than I have cared for any man in my life, and he cares for me. Do not blame your murder of Mr. Wickham on your perception of mine and your brother's feelings for one another." I had never heard such a speech from Jane. Even half that would have been more hateful than she had ever previously been.

"I am sorry, Charles. I simply could not allow it."

"Thankfully, you are not in charge of me, *dear* sister," he replied.

Miss Bingley dissolved into tears and placed herself on one of the seats in the room.

"I am sorry to say it, but we will have to tell the detectives from Scotland Yard what has happened and what Miss Bingley has done," I said delicately.

Mr. Bingley nodded. He seemed shell-shocked, unable to pause the tears that streamed down his face. He was clearly sad for the loss of his sister.

In truth, Miss Bingley had ended not only Mr. Wickham's life that night, but her own, as well.

# CHAPTER SEVEN:
## *The Truth of the Matter*

It was not much longer before the detectives from Scotland Yard came. With Miss Bingley's confession, which had been heard by many more than just a single witness, the case was closed with no further investigation. Whether they would have continued investigating and come to the same conclusion as Mr. Holmes did, should she not have confessed, I do not know, but I doubt that anyone should have been convicted of the murder. If they had convicted anyone, it would have ended up being no more than just a patsy.

Miss Bingley gave up the location of Mr. Hope with ease. They offered her a lesser sentence should she continue to aid the investigation instead of impeding it. Mr. Hope, it turned out, was wanted for multiple murders all over London. He always killed in the same manner and left the same message in blood on the wall for investigators to muddle over.

He had been paid well over the years to kill people for many others. It was a horrible business and I could scarcely believe that there was such high demand for it, but the number of so-called jobs that Mr. Hope had completed was immense. He maintained his innocence, however. He admitted to setting up the murders and accepting money in return for killing, but he truly did not see himself as a murderer. He believed that what he had done was simply move along the will of God. By giving the men he killed a choice between the poisoned pill and the harmless pill, he claimed he had no responsibility if the pill consumed led them to their demise. According to Mr. Holmes, he was suffering from a delusion that caused him to believe that what he had done would not be considered murder, but be considered right and just.

Mr. Bingley still chose to leave Netherfield Park and return to his home in London. Netherfield Park had begun as a haven from the depravity of the city, but it had become a place full of memories the poor man would rather forget.

The death of Mr. Wickham had sparked something in both himself and Jane, though. They both must have felt the pressure of how short life can truly be. They were shy and retiring people, but neither wanted to lose the other. Should Mr. Bingley lose more than his sister as a result of the murder of Mr. Wickham, then I believe he would become a broken, shell of a man. The addition of Mr. Bingley's imminent departure to Jane's and Mr. Bingley's newly confessed love prompted Mr. Bingley to ask Jane to be his wife. I had never seen a woman so happy and should she know more happiness than that, I would be convinced that it should kill her. The only one who could have been known to be happier than Mr. Bingley and Jane at the news of their engagement was Mama.

Mr. Holmes had returned to London with the detectives from Scotland Yard. A new case had begun that they needed assistance on. Mr. Holmes was not keen on the idea of assisting them yet again. In the case of Mr. Wickham, he had simply needed to, as there were no other detectives present to help. I had discovered his usual clients were people who came to visit him in his apartment, private cases. It was rare that he was a consulting detective on an official case. He complained that he would not get credit for solving the case, that the only names to show up in the newspapers would be official policemen and detectives.

I could understand the desire he had for notoriety. He deserved it, but I did not believe he could stay away from a case for the simple reason of vanity. I knew he would take near every case that came his way, if only to prove to himself that he was clever enough to solve it.

I felt the loss of his presence. Lydia was still mending and with her taking up all of Mama's attention, I was able to go about my day almost completely freely. She was more concerned with Lydia's health than with marrying any of her daughters off, at least for the moment. I could not help but feel boredom creep into my daily routine again. The only people I encountered on a regular basis were those that I had known my whole life. I had very little new to learn about them, so my skills in observation were beginning to stagnate. I did not see a way out of these doldrums; they should surely be my own demise. I had developed a fondness for crime solving, deduction, and observation. Without them in my life I had begun to feel an unbearable emptiness.

With Jane gone and Mama tending to Lydia, the house was far too quiet. Kitty spent her days with Lydia, telling her stories and attempting to make her laugh again. Mary continued to practice her piano forte and was improving her talent with every new day. It was just I who felt lost now. I had found my talent and where I belonged, but it was not somewhere a woman was meant to be. Papa could not stand to see me so forlorn. He did everything in his power to raise my spirits, but he could not.

One dewy morning, Papa and I took a stroll through the gardens. After a few silent minutes, he turned to me.

"My dear Lizzy, I had a thought." He smiled mischievously at me. "What if you were to spend some time with Jane and Mr. Bingley in London?"

The true reason for a trip to London was not lost on me. If I went to visit Jane and Mr. Bingley, I could find Mr. Holmes.

So, to London I went, where I would help Mr. Holmes solve his cases and document the most intriguing ones we worked on together. This would be my happily ever after. A partnership of minds, not of marriage, would be my true way to happiness.

FROM THE JANE AUSTEN NOVEL

*Pride & Prejudice*

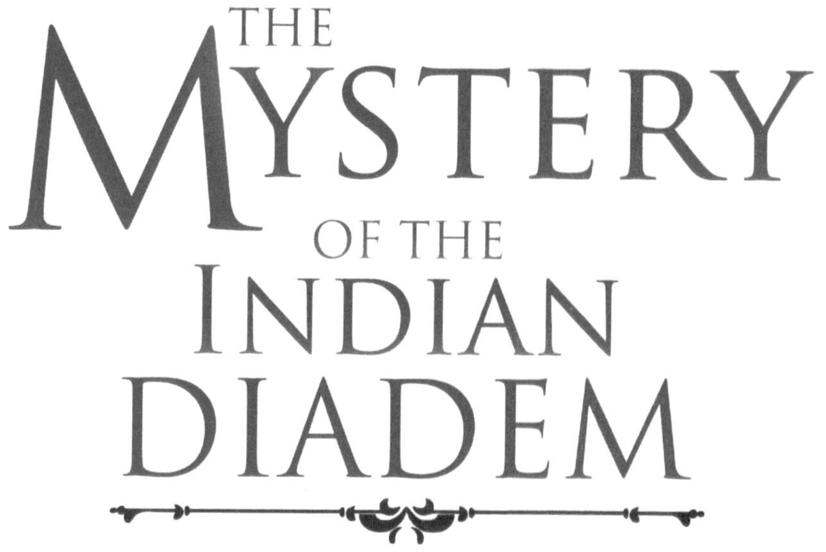

# THE MYSTERY OF THE INDIAN DIADEM

***A Sherlock Holmes & Elizabeth Bennet Mystery***

AMELIA LITTLEWOOD

# CHAPTER ONE:
## A Matter of Family

I had not long resigned myself to life in the countryside without my dear sister Jane before an invitation was extended for me to join her and her new husband in the city. I was grateful for the invitation, for life had become nearly unbearable in Longbourn.

Charlotte Lucas, my closest companion had not long before wed Mr. Collins, of all men. The two became acquainted at the Netherfield Ball where Mr. Wickham had met his untimely end. Though she did not love him, nor could she claim to have even the slightest feelings of affection for the man, she agreed to become his wife. Admittedly she would live well and comfortable, but I was not convinced she would be truly happy. We argued upon her sharing her news with me. Charlotte did not appreciate me judging her for her decision and I could not accept it. I am uncertain that I ever shall, but if it is between my dearest friend and my own stubbornness, I shall choose Charlotte.

Longbourn had become a lonely place, what used to be a haven became a burden. Lydia and Kitty were set to join our aunt and uncle in Derbyshire. Lydia was still affected by her experience with Mr. Wickham, she had lost the sense of innocence she once had. She used to be so light-hearted and boisterous in manner, where now she tended more towards the docile and quiet. It took Mama some convincing to allow her to visit with our aunt and uncle. She was not keen on the idea of Lydia being away from her. Mama's maternal instincts had never been so strong as they were in the wake of Lydia's trauma. This being said, at the close of the day, Lydia and Mama were still themselves and both parties should benefit from time away from one another.

Our aunt and uncle extended the invitation to Mary as well, but she declined, preferring to stay home and practice her piano forte instead. It should be a strange trio left in Longbourn once myself,

Lydia, and Kitty are away. I do wish I could observe Mama, Papa, and Mary as a lonesome trio in our home. I should imagine there to be little talking, which shall drive Mama to the brink of madness.

I could barely wait to leave for London, the city is so diverting compared to the country. It is a good choice that Lydia and Kitty are headed to the countryside, I do not think that either would fare well in the city. Lydia would not yet be able to handle all the excitement of it and Kitty would likely run off with the first scoundrel to lay eyes on her. The countryside's scenery would be different enough from Longbourn to keep them entertained, but not exciting enough for either to ruin the family or themselves. Myself, I needed the excitement that the city would bring. The lull in the wake of Mr. Holmes' absence after the murder of Mr. Wickham had been excruciating. In my time with Mr. Holmes, I had discovered a talent I never would have known I possessed and I could not turn it off though he had been long gone. My mind raced always with observations of human behavior. I could deduce so much from so little. I had discovered so much debauchery within the confines of Longbourn and Meryton that I could not imagine what went on in the city. More than one upstanding citizen was almost certainly having an affair based on my observations and a few others might have a proclivity for opiates.

I hoped to call upon Mr. Holmes once I arrived in London. I thought we made quite a pair solving the murder of Mr. Wickham at the Netherfield Park ball not long ago. Though none of it was proper, I could not bother myself with propriety in this instance. My heart yearned to work with Mr. Holmes and uncover answers once again. It felt as though I myself had an addiction, only I was addicted to solving cases. My nerves were aflutter at the thought of never being able to work in that capacity again. I should perish if my life would remain so dull as it has been these past months.

I had had little correspondence with Mr. Holmes himself since his departure. He had written me once, in response to a letter I sent him. I had made contact with him only to let him know how Lydia was doing and that I should be visiting Jane and Mr. Bingley soon enough. His response was brief. Had it come from any other, it would have been rude. Mr. Holmes' entire message was "*Good.*" His words, or word, rather, gave me hope that I should expect to see him again in the city.

Jane had also updated me more than once about Mr. Holmes. She knew my fascination with the man, and I had confided only in her how much excitement I felt when solving the murder of Mr. Wickham. Dear Jane was the only one I could be open with about how alive Mr. Wickham's untimely demise made me feel, how solving the case of who took his life awoke something within me. It was grizzly and uncouth in every possible way, and Jane was horrified by it when I first confessed it to her. She did not understand how something so terrible could intrigue me so. To be transparent, I did not understand it either and still do not, but I had never felt more alive than I did while uncovering truths about people by observing them. As I spoke with her more, she seemed to accept it without understanding fully. I think it became similar to how I would accept and understand Charlotte's marriage to Mr. Collins over time.

Sweet Jane was in bliss with her dear Mr. Bingley, though she missed her family desperately. She had not been long from home before she begged for me to visit. Mr. Bingley was more than happy to host the entirety of the Bennets in London. I dare say that he should happily do anything that Jane wished of him, he was so in love with her. Jane did think better than to invite all her sisters at once. Mr. Bingley is a dear and never would have complained, but it would certainly be a strain on his good manners to have all his sisters-in-law present in his home for an extended period of time. Jane had been kind enough to invite me to visit knowing that Lydia and Kitty would soon be leaving. She too had reservations about leaving only Mama, Papa, and Mary home, though her concern was genuine where mine was more out of morbid curiosity.

Married life suited Jane well, she was happier than I had ever seen her. Mr. Bingley was also desperately happy, but he had been affected by the death of Mr. Wickham and all that followed. Where he was once light-hearted, there was now a tinge of sadness behind his jovial nature. It was as though the murder of Mr. Wickham had also killed a part of everyone who had been affected by it, with the exception of myself. I had found myself wondering what was wrong with me that the death of another should enliven me. The only solace I had was in Mr. Holmes and the idea that he would not think anything wrong with me, as he came as much alive as I in the wake of tragedy.

I had done some research on Mr. Holmes after his departure. The man was well known in some circles in the city. Mr. Holmes was the first consulting detective in history and worked closely with Scotland Yard on their stranger cases. It appeared as though this was not his primary source of work, though, as Jane informed me he was constantly busy working on private cases. The officers at Scotland Yard only called upon his expertise every few months, but according to Jane and Mr. Bingley, Mr. Holmes was always working, and in many instances, spoke of having to turn away cases. Though I asked where he found his cases, Jane said that she was not sure, and Mr. Bingley confessed that he did not know either. I deduced that he likely took private clients through news advertisements. It would be a far more lucrative method of getting clients than any other. Although Mr. Holmes appeared dishevelled and behaved without manners, I suspected he was raised with wealth and to afford his own bad habits must make a fair amount. The message he had sent me gave me promise that we may meet again upon my arrival in London and I could continue in unfurling the most mysterious subject I had yet to observe.

"Lizzie, do you not think Mary should accompany her sisters to the countryside?" Mama asked while lazing on the couch. Her cheeks were colored from the summer heat and she was fanning herself in an attempt to keep cool. It had been an unusually hot summer thus far. She had been pressing the matter of Mary's refusal to travel with her sisters for the last few days. The oddity of the remaining three Bennets had not been lost on Mama. The relief of having all of her daughters out of the house was not lost on her, either. Mama should be devastated when myself and all my sisters leave for good, but knowing that this was only temporary made her desire the reprieve it would give her.

"I believe that Mary would be surprised to find herself at home in the countryside with our aunt and uncle. I dare say she may even like it better than our own Longbourn," I said without irony. "I think it should be a marvellous thing for Mary to venture into the world." I fully believed this to be true, Mary needed to see more of the world. She was far too accustomed to the walls of Longbourn and had become a hermit at far too young an age. "Though I don't believe her to be flexible or able to be coerced on the matter of going." I added this for my own benefit, as Mama had asked more than once for me to convince Mary to join Lydia and Kitty in the country.

"I suppose you are right in that, Lizzie. Perhaps she may call upon Jane and Mr. Bingley with you on your journey to London." Mama was searching for an excuse to have Mary leave Longbourn with desperation. I could see her nerves growing beneath each statement, threatening a panic.

"I shouldn't think it fair for Mr. Bingley to receive an extra guest upon our arrival. If Mary cannot be convinced to accompany Lydia and Kitty in the country, I doubt that she shall ever agree to join me in the city."

Mama nodded in agreement. We'd had this conversation more than once already this week. The first few times we spoke were much more volatile than this, but it seemed as though she had finally accepted how unlikely it was for Mary to leave Longbourn.

"I suppose you are right in your assumption that having two guests would be more than Mr. Bingley and our dear Jane could handle. They must be so preoccupied with being newlyweds that they have little time for much else."

I made a small sound of agreement in the hope that it would be the end to the conversation.

"You have been so changed, Lizzie, since," Mama trailed off, unsure of how to describe what happened. "Not so much as our poor Lydia, but I have seen a change in you."

"I do not think that anyone in attendance to Mr. Bingley's ball at Netherfield Park left the same as they arrived," I responded.

Mama shook her head sadly, but made no effort to continue the conversation, for which I was grateful. Mama still had her nerves as her greatest companion, but I do believe that she had become an even more wonderful mother because of the incident. She had become more patient, and truthfully, more observant. She could now tell how all her children felt and why by observing them, and where Mama used to be concerned only with her own nerves, she now cared to help us with ours. I knew that I had inherited my observation skills from Mama because of this. It could only be her that gifted me this skill, as our dear Papa was oblivious to human emotion in nature.

My journey to London would begin in just a few days' time. Lydia and Kitty would not leave for another fortnight after. I found myself grateful for this, as my dear sisters could see me off along with Mama and Papa. That was certainly one change in me that I noticed. Where I never felt close with any of my sisters save for dearest Jane, of course, I now cared for them deeply. I do not think I had allowed myself to know them before Mr. Wickham's death. I prejudicially assumed they were simple, silly girls, which I have discovered is not the case. Though they may present that way on the surface, they are incredibly intelligent, thoughtful women. I regret not allowing myself to see them in this manner before.

# CHAPTER TWO:

## *Journey to London*

Mama and Papa desired to hire a private coach for me to travel to London, but I would not hear of it, as it would be far too expensive a trip. It took much convincing for them to allow me to travel by a hired post chaise, but I would prefer it to the solitude of traveling in a private coach. Mail coaches were not made to carry passengers, but they moved people as much as they did mail. Not many preferred a mail coach as a means of travel and, should I have asked, Jane and Mr. Bingley would have chartered a private coach for me. I, however, enjoyed the idea of travel by post chaise, though I had never traveled far that way before. I found myself as excited for the journey as for the destination.

There would be so many incredible and interesting people aboard the mail coach on my journey. I ached to make new observations and few new people came through Meryton and we were so confined to Longbourn that I had no opportunities to deduce and unfurl the true nature of a person I had not already met. The carriage ride to London would be most diverting. Many people that took the post chaise would be characters of all different shapes and sizes. It would be far more interesting than a private coach. I should perish of boredom should I travel all that way alone.

Mama only agreed to my traveling in this manner when Papa told her that I shall fare just as well on a mail coach as a private one. She had become unbearably concerned for our wellbeing after Lydia's attack. It was certainly understandable, but I found it smothering. Papa had finally convinced her that I would be safer in the mail coach than a private one, as there would be more people present should anyone have dubious intentions. In truth, Papa did not care much how I got to London, only that I did arrive there. He was as eager for me to learn more from Mr. Holmes as I and understood without my explaining that the nature of my interest in him was purely platonic. Mama did not understand this and worried that Mr. Holmes and I might develop a romantic interest in one another. Personally, I do not think Mr. Holmes to even be capable of such emotions.

The trip ended up being uneventful, to my displeasure. The post chaise was late arriving in Meryton. Mama complained the entire way into town, the idea that we had to carry my belongings into town for me to travel in such a manner humiliated her. She could not abide by it for my return trip and insisted that I request Mr. Bingley and Jane charter a private coach for my journey home.

In the wake of my trip on the mail carriage to London, I did not much mind the thought of traveling back in luxury. I underestimated how uncomfortable the seating would be and even though we paid extra for me to sit inside the carriage rather than on top, it was not a comfortable journey. The seats were barely cushioned and left me sore all over as we journeyed over uneven roads. We got stuck in the mud for a short amount of time after the weather took a turn and it began to pour down with rain. All the passengers had to evacuate the carriage and the men were required to help push it out of the mud.

As I was inside of the post chaise with only three other people, I was unable to utilize my observation skills in the way I desired to. My plan was to sharpen my skills prior to meeting with Mr. Holmes, but I did not get as much of a chance as I had expected. My three companions in the carriage were interesting enough to observe, but were not difficult to analyze.

There was a young man and a woman traveling together, not older than myself. Clearly, they were unmarried and had chosen to run away together. Their families disapproved of their union for many reasons, I am certain. There are always reasons to object to a union when love is the primary force between merging two individuals. The typical reason for objection was financial: one side of the match was not financially comfortable. Another might be that one party is already promised to another they hardly know. Just as likely, the parents simply do not approve of the match for their child. I applauded the two for choosing love above all else, but could not imagine the shame such an elopement would bring to their families.

The third companion was a gentleman in his later years. He was very private. He kept to himself most of the journey. Everything about him implied that he was secretive and closed off. He sat angling his body towards the window, away from the other passengers and he hunched his shoulders to be further obscured from us. I never got a good look at his face the entire journey. I found his behavior most odd and intriguing. His clothing was far nicer than would be expected for one riding a mail carriage for travel. His garb expressed to me that he was wealthier than even Mr. Bingley. He hugged a trunk to his chest that read "Morton" in gold lettering. He held it so tightly to his chest that his knuckles went white. What the case held inside was likely the man's most treasured possession and he was concerned for its safety. Judging by his cagey behavior, he had concerns for his own safety, as well. I spent most of the journey in the carriage watching the man, as the couple were not nearly as interesting as he.

Jane enveloped me in a large hug as I stepped off the carriage. I had told her not to bother waiting on me to arrive, that I should be fine meeting her at her home. She did not listen to my words though, as she had stood waiting for me for a time before the mail carriage finally arrived.

"I did not want you to get lost on your way," Jane insisted.

I did not believe it for a moment. She could not contain her excitement to see me nor could I. In truth, I could not have been happier to see her when I stepped out of the post chaise. Jane's face lit up when she saw me. She had always been the most beautiful Bennet daughter, but her happiness with Mr. Bingley had made her even more radiant.

"My dear Lizzie, I have missed you so," Jane said, squeezing my hand in hers. Her smile seemed to warm me from the cold.

"Dearest Jane, you look more beautiful than ever. Married life suits you."

Jane blushed at my compliment and shook her head in disagreement, but knew me better than to argue.

I continued, "I confess I am glad you waited on the coach, for I may have been lost forever should I try to navigate the city on my own."

"I too found it difficult to navigate when I first arrived, but it has become home after quite an adjustment."

She linked her arm in mine as we walked down the busy street towards hers and Mr. Bingley's home. It was a magnificent sight. The city was more compact than I had remembered, I had visited only once before and it was long before I had an appreciation for the world around me. Mr. Bingley's and Jane's home was glorious, larger than any other on the street. The tall arched door was black with gold hardware showing the house number as 110. The inside of the home was even more impressive than the out. The floors were tiled with marble and black tiles in a fashionable pattern. A massive staircase invited you up to the second floor.

"Your home is lovely," I said, awestruck by the opulence of my sister's residence.

I knew how wealthy Mr. Bingley was and had seen the incredible beauty of Netherfield Park, but the aesthetics of their city estate made Netherfield Park look like a humble country abode. The entire estate was fitted with the most expensive and fashionable products. It pleased me to know that Jane lived in such comfort. I knew that the extreme luxury of her new life had been difficult for her to adjust to and the estate had not felt like home instantly. I was happy to know that she had begun to feel at home in her new position. She had to be the kindest head of house there ever was. The men and women in her and Mr. Bingley's employ should be grateful of their kind and generous natures. I imagine that if a position could be fought over it would have been to work in the home of dear Jane and Mr. Bingley. I had once joked with Mama that the two of them would go through his yearly four thousand pounds by doing no more than giving it all away. She was horrified at the very thought of that, but understood my meaning that Mr. Bingley and Jane were simply too generous for their own good.

"Ah, Ms. Bennet, it is so wonderful to see you again," Mr. Bingley said with a bow. He softly embraced Jane, and chided her, "I did not know that you were meeting our dear Elizabeth at the coach."

Jane smiled at him broadly, though his tone was laced with concern for her well-being.

"I thought I might get lost on my journey to your most impressive estate," I replied, and as an afterthought, because it felt strange to hear my full name in use, though it was my proper name: "You may call me Lizzie, Mr. Bingley. We are family after all." I realized the irony of my statement before it had even crossed my lips.

"And you, Lizzie, must call me Charles."

I nodded with a smile in agreement, though it would be something to adjust to. Jane and Mr. Bingley had left so soon for London after their marriage that we had not long been acquainted with him as our brother-in-law and still only knew him as Mr. Bingley.

"Has our dearest Jane shared our wonderful news with you?"

"No, I thought we should tell her together," Jane interjected before I could ask what he was referring to.

She walked to Mr. Bingley and gripped his hand. The two were looking at me with excitement.

"What news is this, pray tell me!" I could not think what they wanted to share with me as a unit.

"I am with child," Jane announced, breaking into a grin and then bursting into joyous laughter.

I did not know how to reply to such incredible news and all I could do was pull Jane into my arms tightly and laugh with her. Mr. Bingley stood to the side and although I may have imagined it, I thought he might have tears brimming in his eyes. Jane broke from the hug and gripped my hands.

"We want you to be the godmother," she added, and it was my turn to begin tearing up.

I hugged Jane again, still at a loss for words. "Have you told anyone else thusly?" I asked, knowing the answer must be no, for if any of our sisters or Mama had been told, the news would no longer be a secret.

Jane shook her head and embraced me again, her excitement too large to contain.

# CHAPTER THREE:

## Mr Holmes and I

After hearing the wonderful news, I nearly wanted to remain by Jane's side for the duration of my time in London. Likely she would have been more than happy to have me as a constant companion in my time there, but she was kind enough to know my ulterior motives for visiting her. Jane would not allow me to neglect my own desires to call upon Mr. Holmes because of her. I couldn't believe that I hadn't known she was with child the moment I'd seen her. As every day passed I could see her grow rounder with the child inside her. I did not want to leave her side, but she could be as stubborn as I, and after near a week visiting reminded me of my other reason for being in the city with her.

"Dear Lizzie, you could remain by my side for the rest of your stay and I should be happier than I have ever been before, but the pair of us both know that neither would be satisfied with this arrangement," Jane said as she sat across from me in the parlour room.

"I do not know what you mean, Jane," I responded, though I did know her exact meaning.

"We both know that you should call upon Mr. Holmes while you are in the city. It would be a great disappointment to both of you should you not and I shall feel guilty if you do not go on my account."

I crossed the room to sit next to my dear sister. "I do not want to leave you or my godchild," I said in earnest. It was the truth. No matter how tempting meeting with Mr. Holmes could be, I had no doubt in my mind that I would prefer to remain with Jane.

"I know that you do not, but when you are on your way back to Longbourn, I should think that you would not feel the same as you do now. I know you, Lizzie, and I know that you wish to remain with me and the babe. However, you will regret it forever should you not see Mr. Holmes again."

I knew that she was correct in her assessment. Although Jane did not have my skill for deduction or observation, she knew me well and understood every piece of my being.

"I suppose you are correct, though I do not know if the man even desires to see me," I admitted.

Jane laughed at this comment, though I did not see the humor in it. "He shall be grateful for a visit from you, my dear Lizzie."

Jane insisted that I take the carriage to Mr. Holmes' apartment on Baker Street. She did not feel it safe for me to walk all the way there from their estate. She did not think that it was a good area for a young woman to be alone, especially one of good standing. Though I doubted her concerns were valid, I acquiesced and took the carriage. Mama had been shocked that Mr. Holmes lived in an apartment and had befriended someone so high standing as Mr. Bingley. Her prejudice against apartments, I felt, influenced the rest of us and this was the true reason for Jane's concerns.

The ride was shorter than I had expected. I exited the carriage and told the driver the time I expected to be leaving.

I was given a shock when I rang the doorbell to apartment 221B Baker Street and a woman answered the door. I felt sure that I had gotten the address incorrect. She was not a young woman, but not yet old. She smiled at me as she opened the door.

"How can I help you, dear?" she asked.

"I am looking for Mr. Holmes," I responded tentatively, unsure that I had come to the correct place.

She nodded enthusiastically and told me to come in as she herded me in through the doorway. "I'm Mrs. Hudson, his landlady."

It amazed me that this woman owned the home that we were currently standing in, but I had barely a moment to think that over before she was gesturing to the staircase.

"The entrance is just up those stairs," she clarified with a grin, her ruddy cheeks like apples.

"Thank you," I said.

As I began up the stairs, I could hear voices behind the entry door to Mr. Holmes' apartment. I worried that I had come at a poor time and he already had visitors. Given his antisocial nature, it surprised me that he not be alone most of the time. The way that Mrs. Hudson answered the door and had no reaction when I said that my reason for being there was to visit Mr. Holmes expressed to me that he often had people call upon him. I wondered if it were clients that so regularly came through that door. He must have many of them to afford to live in such a place with no other source of income. Though he lived in an apartment, it was no small building and it appeared to be almost as stylish as Mr. Bingley's and Jane's home.

I stood at the top of the stairs in front of Mr. Holmes' door, unsure of how to proceed. I could certainly hear voices behind the door and did not want to intrude, but I had already sent the carriage away. I may have turned back and returned to Jane, but busy worrying about the dilemma I was in, I did not notice his door swing open. A couple of gentlemen left the apartment, each of them giving a friendly nod my way. Mr. Holmes was not among them, and the door swung shut as the men exited. I went to the door and knocked three times.

"Yes. Come in," Mr. Holmes barked from inside the apartment. He sounded annoyed by the intrusion, but not as if it was unexpected to have someone knocking on his door. I creaked the door open, knowing that it was not me that Mr. Holmes expected to be calling upon him.

"Pleasure to see you again, Mr. Holmes," I said as I entered the apartment fully. To my own surprise, Mr. Holmes did not appear surprised that I called upon him at all. He smiled from a large armchair that was place opposite the door as I walked into the room. There was a sofa set up across from the chair where he sat. "You do not seem surprised to see me."

"You told me that you would call upon me when you visited your sister and Mr. Bingley. It was only a matter of when you would arrive. As your sister is with child, I knew that you would spend the first part of your trip by her side. She means more to you than any other person. It was simply a matter of time before she urged you to visit me, as she understands that visiting her was not the only reason for your trip to London."

Mr. Holmes enjoyed showing off his observation skills and though it impressed me, I did find it somewhat irritating. It was impressive that he knew of Jane's expectancy, but it did not surprise me that he had figured it out, although it did cross my mind that Mr. Bingley had told him and he was only pretending to have deduced it.

"Well, it is nice to see you," I responded. Mr. Holmes had not stood from his seat to greet me, though I did not expect him to. His sense of propriety was near non-existent, which was a reprieve for me. I found it refreshing to not have to worry about manners or how I acted around Mr. Holmes. I was much repressed in my day-to-day life because of concerns with manners and propriety. I settled myself on the sofa and asked, "How did you know that my sister was with child?"

"I am pleased that you have called upon me at last," Mr. Holmes replied. "In truth, Mr. Bingley told me the happy news not long after your arrival."

I smiled to myself, happy both that he was not all-knowing and that he had told me the truth. It was refreshing and further promoted the candor in our odd companionship.

“I knew that you would call upon me, but you have chosen a most exciting time to visit. Did you see those gentlemen who left before you came in?” he prompted.

“I did see them, yes. I assume that they were clients?”

Mr. Holmes nodded.

“Did they give you an exciting case to work on?” I queried.

"No, they were complete fools. Idiots. Their case was easily solved. I did not even have to leave the room to figure it out." He rolled his eyes at the stupidity of the men.

“What was their case?” I asked with curiosity. I had been so distanced from the world of crime solving that I was starved for any amount of mystery in my life.

Mr. Holmes sighed. “The men were brothers-in-law looking for their sister and wife, respectively. Without so much as a few words I understood immediately where the woman was. She had been forced to marry her husband for the monetary gain, but was in love with another man, a poor man, and had since run away with him. The brother knew all of this, but covered for her because he did not want her husband to know what happened for fear of retaliation. The husband is a very powerful man in London and feared by many.

"The brother pretended to be concerned with her safety and suggested that they both hire a private detective to uncover her whereabouts. Unfortunately for him, they came to me. I was able to deduce all of this from their telling of the events and the brother's truth came out. The husband nearly killed the man for hiding the truth of where the woman was, but after a while the two of them were able to calm down and left in relative harmony. Though I assume the husband will retaliate. I should put in a word at Scotland Yard to keep an eye out for the both of them."

I could feel my own heart beat faster as he went on explaining the case and my thoughts began to race when he got to the end. "I wonder what he will do to the brother," I said with slight horror.

Mr. Holmes did not seem concerned. He lacked a certain level of empathy that most others observed.

"I am sure nothing good," Mr. Holmes replied flippantly. "Her husband is the leader of a feared and revered gang in the city. The brother will probably not survive the night, and more than likely, nothing shall happen to the husband, as he has many important people in his pocket."

I shuddered at the thought. There was so much more debauchery than I had expected in the city, and with this case alone. "Should you not do something to protect him, then?"

Mr. Holmes shrugged and shook his head.

"If he is to die, at least give him warning so he may protect himself," I insisted, horrified at Mr. Holmes' casual attitude towards the looming murder of an innocent man.

Mr. Holmes seemed to be getting irritated. "The man is already aware of his fate and stepping in to protect him is not my duty and should I do that, it would put myself in immense danger and those close to me, as well. Though I do not have many friends or family, the ones I do have are dear to me and I do not wish to put them in danger because a man lied and allowed his sister to run off with a man for love even though she belonged to another already. The man knew exactly what he was doing."

The statement was sharp and unforgiving. I did not agree completely, but I understood why he would not want to be involved further with such a dangerous man. The friends he spoke of that would be in danger included the people closest to me and I would be most unhappy should any misfortune befall them.

"I suppose you are right. I apologize if I have offended. I did not understand why you were uninterested in helping the man, but I see why now. I am unused to the harsh ways of the city. I have never come across such things in my life."

Mr. Holmes shook his head. "Do not apologize for causing offense. You simply spoke your mind. It is true that I could do something to save the man's life, but I will do nothing and he will die. It is a terrible truth of life that you must weigh options such as these." He seemed for a moment to be much older than his years. He shook the emotion from himself and straightened his back in his seat. "The reason why I said you have come at such a fortunate time is that the next client who shall be visiting us is very interesting with an intriguing case that I am hopeful will take more than a few moments to solve."

Mr. Holmes' excitement for the macabre made me feel more at home than I felt in my own household. No one there had understood why I had been so enlivened when solving the murder of Mr. Wickham. They thought it ghastly of me. At 221B Baker Street, this was not the case.

"Who is the client?" I asked, positioning myself to one end of the sofa so that another person could sit by me.

"A young woman by the name of Mary Morton."

The name seemed oddly familiar to me, although I could not at the time place where I had heard it before. Her case must have been of extreme intrigue for Mr. Holmes, as he remembered the name of the client. In his retelling of the gang leader and his brother-in-law, not a single name was ever mentioned. I knew him well enough to know that this was not to give them privacy, it was simply because Mr. Holmes did not care enough to recall their names.

Mr. Holmes knew very little about his cases or clients before he met with them in person. They often sent him letters with little details about their cases, and their name. If he found it of enough interest, he would agree to meet with them at 221B Baker Street. If that small amount of detail was enough to incite this level of intrigue in Mr. Holmes, I could not imagine what the case must be.

"What do you know of her case thus far?"

Mr. Holmes grinned at me with the gleeful look of a child awakened on Christmas morning. "Absolutely nothing," he replied without a hint of irony.

"You know nothing about Ms. Morton's case?" I clarified.

"Not one detail of it. Ms. Morton claims that it is far too dangerous to put anything in writing, and I want to know what has her so fearful."

# CHAPTER FOUR:
## *The Devil is in the Details*

Ms. Morton arrived not much after Mr. Holmes introduced her case to me, what little of it he had. She had been vague in her letter even about when she would call upon Mr. Holmes. Ms. Morton was fearful for her life and did not want to give anyone who might intercept her letter to Mr. Holmes details they would need to learn of her whereabouts.

She had used a code in her letter that she knew that Mr. Holmes would be able to translate. It was simple and anyone who inspected the letter thoroughly would have been able to deduce what it was. She had simply darkened the letters and numbers that she wanted him to read. When written together the letters read: *Thursday at 2 in the afternoon*. Aside from the bolded letters, the message seemed like a simple note asking how Mr. Holmes was doing, as if the two were old friends and she wanted to catch up with him.

Mr. Holmes was intrigued and impressed with the woman and her case. Not many would think to use such a code even if they did fear for their lives. He had been initially put off by how familiar the letter was in its manner. It read as a dull message between friends, and Mr. Holmes had been confused by it, knowing that he had never before met Ms. Morton. When he finally inspected the message closer, he unravelled the mystery of it.

Ms. Morton seemed pleased when she entered the room and realized that her message did not go undiscovered.

"Mr. Holmes, it is a pleasure to meet you," she said, extending her hand to him. It was an odd gesture to see a woman make, but Mr. Holmes shook her hand in greeting without realizing the strangeness of it. "I assume you understood my message."

"A pleasure, Ms. Morton. I did deduce your coded message, ma'am." He was not as impressed with the code itself as he was with the concept of a woman so fearful that she felt that she had to code her messages for worry of being hunted down. "Please, be seated." He gestured to the spot open next to me.

I bowed my head in greeting. "I'm Elizabeth Bennet, an associate of Mr. Holmes."

I had not thought of how to introduce myself, and stumbled on how to describe my relationship with Mr. Holmes. Associate seemed more accurate than acquaintance or even friend.

She paused, looking at me with scrutiny.

"You understand the nature of my fear, Mr. Holmes." She turned, addressing Mr. Holmes, ignoring my presence. "Is she to be trusted?"

"She has helped me solve cases in the past. She is my most trusted associate," Mr. Holmes replied with a imperceptible glimmer of a smile on his lips. Though he pluralized the number of cases we had worked together in the past, I was happy that he trusted me in this matter.

"I do hope so." Ms. Morton took the seat beside me. It was clear that she was nervous as she continually looked over her shoulder at the door as though she expected someone to barge through it at any moment. "I have never been one for paranoia, but I do know that if I should let my guard down, it will mean my life. Perhaps I should return when you are not accompanied by anyone, Mr. Holmes."

Ms. Morton stood and turned to leave the room. It was at that moment the familiarity of her name made sense to me.

"Ms. Morton!" I exclaimed, making her pause.

Mr. Holmes had been about to begin speaking and did not take kindly to my interruption, but I needed to say what was in my mind. I also knew that it would convince her to trust in me and to stay so that Mr. Holmes and I could work the case together.

"I am sorry, Ms. Bennet, it is nothing the matter with you. I simply cannot trust many people right now."

I stood from my seat, as well. "I understand, Ms. Morton, but I think I may know why you are here already."

She stood, open-mouthed. I could see the terror in her eyes as she went over every possible moment leading up to her arrival to see if she had done something foolish to betray her story.

It was when she turned that I made the connection. I remembered the strange man on the mail coach angling himself in the same way she did as she turned to leave the room. The similarity in their faces was undeniable and I could see her mannerisms aligning with those of the man who had traveled with me. He too had been cagey and suspicious, paranoid even.

"What do you mean?" she asked finally. Her terror was palpable. She was just as easily to assume Mr. Holmes and I were secretly assassins hired to bring about her death as two people wanting to offer assistance.

"Did your father recently travel by post chaise to London?" I asked.

Mr. Holmes had remained silent through our conversation, though he seemed mildly surprised when I said I knew why she was there. He could not be enjoying our back and forth any more. His head whipped between us as though he were watching a tennis match.

Ms. Morton gasped and sunk back to her seat beside me. "How did you know that?" she asked and I knew that we had her.

She could have assumed that we had killed her father and that was why we knew his whereabouts, but thankfully she did not jump to this incorrect assumption. I could not explain why I knew that her father had been murdered and that was why she had come to Mr. Holmes. I would like to believe it was observation or deduction that brought me to that conclusion, but I am not so sure. Mr. Morton had given me such an unpleasant feeling, I believe that I could feel that he was a dead man walking when we rode in the mail carriage together.

"I believe I traveled with him in the same post chaise. He had already been riding for some time when I boarded and got off ahead of me." I had not made the connection with the name because Mr. Morton had not gotten off in London. It made sense to me now that he was simply covering his tracks from whoever it was he was hiding from. He did not get off in London because he did not want anyone knowing that he was in the city. "He had with him a trunk with your name printed on it."

Ms. Morton nodded, looking forlorn. "He had gone to the country to collect something, but he would not tell me what. When he returned, he acted stranger than I had ever seen him. He had been jumpy for a long time. He suffered after his return from military duty. He could not recover from the horrors he witnessed. He was scarred in more ways than one from his tour of duty. It was not strange for him to act as though he thought someone was following him or watching him, but in the months leading up to and the days following his trip, it got much worse than it had been.

"He believed that someone was following him and that they wanted to kill him. My brother and I always thought that he was simply crazed from his time in the war, that he had become so accustomed to having a threat around every corner that he could not adjust to normal life after his return. It was not until I went to visit him the other day that I believed his fears to be true." Ms. Morton let out a sob as she finished this statement.

"Your father was murdered," Mr. Holmes interjected.

Ms. Morton nodded and I placed a comforting hand on her shoulder in an attempt to soothe the poor woman.

"My brother does not believe that his death was intentional, but I do."

The question of his death being possibly of natural causes made me wonder how he met his demise. It reminded me of how Mr. Wickham was killed. A simple pill could induce the death of a man, leaving hardly any evidence behind. If her father's death was anything like that, her brother would not be a fool for thinking the death to be natural. Mr. Morton had appeared elderly enough when we traveled together and as he had been in the war, he had to be aged quite a bit.

"Why do you doubt the cause of your father's demise?" Mr. Holmes asked. He was as intrigued as myself.

"The doctor ruled it an accident. It appeared as though he fell and hit his head. I went to visit him to ensure that he was alright, but when I arrived I found him lying in his own blood on the floor of his office. He was an elderly man and walked with a limp ever since the war. It would not take a leap of the imagination to rule his death accidental if it appeared he fell."

"But you do not believe that he fell." Mr. Holmes was not asking a question, but rather making a statement.

"I know that he did not fall," she said with an amount of certainty that I am not sure I have felt in my entire life. "My brother believes what he believes because he cannot face the truth. I can. My father was murdered and now my life is being threatened and I need you to find out who is behind this."

Mr. Holmes and myself remained silent at her forceful delivery.

"I can pay you both handsomely," she added hastily.

"Why do you doubt, though?" Mr. Holmes asked. This had been the information he'd wanted Ms. Morton to disclose in the first place and I too had realized that she had not answered it. I was also curious to know in what way her own life had been threatened and why her life and not her brother's.

"He had been so paranoid these last few months, he wrote to me on his journey telling me that he was sure to be killed upon his return to London. I urged him to come home, believing his fears to be unwarranted. Somehow, I convinced him to return and only a few days later he met his end. The timing is far too suspicious for this to have been an accident. Then, I received this in the mail only a day after his death." She handed Mr. Holmes a piece of paper with a message scrawled across it in nearly illegible handwriting.

He read aloud: "'*Miss Morton, your father was killed because he did not return what is rightfully mine. He knew what he took from me and refused to do the right thing and return it. You now have the opportunity to do the right thing and return that which is rightfully mine. Should you take the same course as your father, you shall meet the same fate as he.*'" Mr. Holmes squinted through some parts, unable to read them clearly, as the handwriting was so poor. "Did you show this to your brother?"

I wondered the same thing. Had her brother seen the message, he could not rightfully believe that his father died of natural causes.

"I showed it to him as soon as I received it," she responded fretfully. "He does not believe its authenticity. He is of the mind that whoever sent the letter to me was a scoundrel looking for me to relinquish to them our inheritance or some large sum of money."

"Do you know what the author of the letter is referring to about what your father had that belonged to them?" I queried.

I did not for a moment believe her brother's theory. It would be far too well-planned if her father's death was an accident, and the language the author of the message used was strange. They repeated that what her father had belonged to them multiple times. If they were simply looking for ransom in exchange for not taking Ms. Morton's life, they would have used different wording.

"I have not even the faintest idea. We have money, but my father worked hard his whole life to build a textile mill that did very well for itself. Nothing that we have is from anything but his hard work," Ms. Morton said. She was obviously offended at the mere thought of her father having taken from someone else to line his own pockets.

"Perhaps the author was not speaking of money," I offered.

Mr. Holmes scoffed at this comment. "It is always about money," he said with a heavy sigh. "It is a dull and uninspired motivation, but it will do."

I worried that this comment would offend Ms. Morton and Mr. Holmes had insulted her father's death. She either did not mind or did not notice, as she made no comment.

"Do not fool yourself, Miss Elizabeth, for it will always be about love or money." His comment dripped with disdain.

"If it is about money, is it possible your father may have been involved in something that you were unaware of?" I asked, ignoring Mr. Holmes.

Ms. Morton shook her head. "I have been running the business from behind the curtains, so to speak, for years now. My father could no longer handle it with his failing health and growing paranoia. My brother had no interest in the family business and gladly acted as the face of the mill without having to handle any of the books."

Ms. Morton was an impressive woman by all standards, and very progressive in every way, it appeared. Whoever threatened her had to be privy to the fact that she had been in charge of the family business and not her brother. For them to threaten her over her brother meant that they probably knew that she had access to the numbers and her brother did not.

"My brother does not truly believe in his own theories or that father's death was an accident, he simply chooses to pretend that this is the case. He has never been one to deal with hard truths and this is the hardest truth we shall ever come across. He cannot accept that we dismissed our father's concerns for so long only to have them turn out to be real.

"He urged our father, along with myself, to return to the city. He had left for the country in a rush, claiming that he had to get something, but he was gone for a long while. In his correspondence, the paranoia seemed to worsen to a point where he could hardly function. My brother and I both felt that he would fare better in the city with us by his sides. It never occurred to either of us that his worries were valid."

Ms. Morton began to tear up. She was a strong woman and had refused to cry until this point. I admired her strength, knowing that I would have sobbed much sooner and she still only allowed a few tears to fall.

"Do you have any idea what your father did in the country?" Mr. Holmes asked.

"He stayed with a friend of his from the war. They served together. I have no idea what he could have been holding onto for my father all these years."

She seemed at a complete loss. Her father's life had been taken because he refused to return something that did not belong to him, or so it would seem. Now the responsibility fell on her shoulders to return it or she would have to pay the ultimate price. The problem was that she had no idea what she was meant to return. Everyone around her was certain that she had begun to go as mad as her father, and did not believe her claims. I could not imagine how difficult the entire situation must have been for her. Even her own brother questioned her sanity.

In a near whisper, she admitted, "I regret more than anything bringing my father home."

My heart broke for the woman and the guilt that she would carry with her for the rest of her time.

"Bringing your father home did not kill him. Whoever wrote you this letter did," Mr. Holmes said with more empathy than I had ever seen him express before. "Miss Elizabeth and I shall take your case, of course."

"I am honored to help uncover the truth of your father's passing," I said to Ms. Morton.

She smiled at me, tears still brimming in her eyes.

"I have to ask; do you know the whereabouts of your father's case? The one he carried with him on the journey." I was certain that the mysterious belonging that caused all of this was contained in that case. I recalled how closely he held the trunk to his chest, the whites of his knuckles as he gripped it tightly.

"Thank you both," she said warmly. "I do know where the case is. It should be in my father's study. It was there when I found his body. The police took an inventory just in case of a robbery."

"Could you bring that to us at our next meeting?" I requested.

Ms. Morton nodded, understanding my assumption, though she did not seem as interested in the line of investigation. From her disposition, I assumed that perhaps she knew it was empty, and had checked it after having the same thought as I had. She did not hint at whether this was correct or not.

She simply adjusted her manner and began negotiating the cost of hiring the pair of us.

After a lengthy discussion that I had no part of, the price was set and we had been hired as private detectives. After this, Mr. Holmes and I ushered her out the door, saying our goodbyes and assuring her that we would find the culprit responsible for her father's death and for threatening her life.

# CHAPTER FIVE:

## Foul Trickery

A change had occurred within me not long after my meeting with Mr. Holmes and Ms. Morton. I no longer wanted to be by Jane's side at all times. In fact, my time with her and Mr. Bingley became a chore, which I hate to admit. I cherished both of them and their unborn child and it was not that they were the reason my time with them had become so unbearable, the fault was entirely mine. I could find no interest in our conversation, I had no desire to eat or even to sleep. My only thoughts were of Ms. Morton and her father. I became obsessed with solving their case. Near every day I chartered Jane's private carriage and returned to 221B Baker Street to investigate with Mr. Holmes.

Jane noticed my shift in behavior and instead of being upset by it, encouraged me to continue working with Mr. Holmes. She beamed with pride when I told her that I would earn money from working this case. It was not long ago that I confided in her how little my desire to marry had become. Observing Ms. Morton and Mrs. Hudson and their independence made me want my own. They both succeeded in earning their own fortunes and lived comfortably off their own labor. I wanted to do the same.

My initial belief was that Ms. Morton's brother was behind, at the very least, the threatening letters. Mr. Morton had left very little behind to his son, fairly leaving the business and most of its assets to Ms. Morton. If his father had slipped and fell, upon realizing how little he would get, her brother might have sent a letter to Ms. Morton demanding that which was rightfully his. As the sole male heir to their father's fortune, it would make sense that he should believe that the mill and all its assets belonged to him. It would also explain why he did not share his sister's concerns about the letter. It would also be plausible to believe that her brother had killed their father in a fit of rage if he had discovered how little he would be left with and was humiliated because his sister was far more successful than he.

Upon looking further into her brother, Mr. Edward Morton, however, it became clear that he did not have the mental capacity to come up with such a complex plan. Not that he was a half-wit, but when we observed him, we realized that his sister was being kind saying that he did not want to take over the family business. It was clear that he did not have the acumen to do so. It appeared that his only hobbies were gambling, drinking, and women—and he liked it that way. Mr. Holmes and I quickly removed him as a suspect.

Mr. Holmes seemed almost gleeful that it was not her brother. “Too easy,” was his comment when I theorized that her brother might have been behind it all. It was almost maniacal, the way he desired for cases to be more complicated and difficult to solve. Mr. Holmes was more intelligent than the rest of the world, it seemed, and this was both a blessing and a curse. He found life to be so mundane and dull when not solving a complex puzzle that he did not enjoy it any other time.

Our only lead aside from the younger Mr. Morton was the man that the senior Mr. Morton had been visiting in the country. Ms. Morton gave us his address so that we could contact him. His name was Sir Fredrick Howard, and he had served in the military at the same time as Mr. Morton had. I researched the name and discovered him to be a highly decorated war veteran. He had saved many lives and taken many more to receive the honors that he did. Sir Howard had been Mr. Morton's commanding officer when they served in the war together.

I wrote to him with haste as soon as Ms. Morton gave us his information. I simply explained that Mr. Morton had died under suspicious circumstances and because of those circumstances we needed to know why Mr. Morton had visited him in the country. I hoped that Sir Howard was familiar enough with Mr. Morton to know of his deep-rooted paranoia and that he would assist us in our investigation.

The threat of the initial letter hung over the investigation like a dark cloud. Ms. Morton seemed barely to have slept since our first encounter and she had grown thinner, as well. Her dark eyes jumped around each room she entered, as if she believed every moment to be her last.

Although she was eager for us to find the culprit, Ms. Morton almost had us out when we interviewed her brother. She would not abide by our suspicions, and in fact, found the accusation offensive, but after explaining to her that we must look from every angle when investigating a crime, she understood. I privately explained to her that the culprit of the last investigation Mr. Holmes and I worked ended up being a close relative of a friend. Mr. Holmes would not approve of me sharing such private information with a client, but I knew that Ms. Morton needed the extra information in order to wholly accept our reasons for questioning her brother. Still, she urged us to forget about her brother as a suspect and focus on what her father had been doing in the country with Sir Fredrick Howard. She was quite relieved and not a bit surprised when we reached the same conclusion as she had.

Ms. Morton allowed us into her father's study to investigate the place where he was allegedly murdered, although she refused to return to the scene with us. Once we arrived, it was clear why.

The study itself was a nice room, lined with bookshelves made of dark wood. In the center was a desk of the same wood. There were two comfortable looking chairs set up across from the desk and one intimidating looking one behind. It was a sparsely decorated room with nearly no ornaments or trinkets to make it appear homey.

It was clear where Mr. Morton had fallen. One of the massive book shelves had a large break in the wood. It was splintered in all directions and caked in thick, dry blood. The carpet beneath the broken book case was disfigured by a dark red stain. The horror that must have befallen Ms. Morton as she entered her father's study was unimaginable and it was no wonder she chose not to revisit it.

In the corner, underneath the window, lay Mr. Morton's case. It was circular in shape with a flat bottom so that it could stand without falling. It was a rich black leather and the gold lettering was just as I remembered it. I went to the case, which I noted was in an odd spot.

"This was the case I saw Mr. Morton holding on the journey to London. He did not set it down once. His grip was so tight on it that his knuckles turned to white. Whatever it is he visited the country to retrieve it must be inside this case."

I had spoken with Ms. Morton about the case briefly. She did not recall her father treating it with such importance before his departure. Mr. Holmes and I believed that Mr. Morton had visited Sir Howard to retrieve whatever it was that his killer desired to be returned. I opened the case expectantly, but was disappointed, as the inside was completely empty.

"I am not surprised by this outcome, but had hoped for better, Miss Elizabeth," Mr. Holmes said solemnly, looking into the empty case over my shoulder.

I was visibly underwhelmed by the empty case. In truth, I had been interested in the contents of Mr. Morton's case even before we were hired by his daughter to investigate his murder. The entire journey on the mail carriage all I could think of was what might be inside of the case Mr. Morton was holding so tightly.

I sighed. “I am not either. Ms. Morton insisted that the case was empty before we arrived, and it appears as though she was correct.”

Ms. Morton had peeked inside the case after her father’s death, as she had noticed it in the study when she found his body. It was an odd room for it to be in and even stranger was where it was placed. Her instincts told her that the case had some important bearing on her father’s death, but she too was disappointed to find it was empty.

Mr. Holmes stood staring at the broken book shelf for a long while. I knew better than to interrupt him while he was deep in thought, so I explored the rest of the room, looking for any bit of evidence that pointed to the death of Mr. Morton being foul play. Though both Mr. Holmes and I believed that Ms. Morton was telling the truth, there had not yet been any solid evidence that pointed to Mr. Morton’s death being purposeful aside from the letter.

“Mr. Morton was almost certainly pushed,” Mr. Holmes declared at last. He had been standing without movement for quite some time and I was beginning to become concerned with his well-being.

"How can you be sure?" I asked, making my way back towards the broken book shelf where Mr. Holmes stood.

"Observe," he ordered, placed his hands on my shoulders, and moved me to where he had been standing.

I squinted, trying to see what it was that Mr. Holmes had deduced. How he expected me to come to a conclusion in moments when he stood there for near an hour, I do not know.

"You are trying too hard, Miss Elizabeth. You need to block out all other thoughts and just focus on what is in front of your face."

I nodded, trying to clear my mind.

Mr. Holmes had been working with me, almost training me in his way of thinking. I had begun to realize that although Mr. Holmes seemed to host a world of knowledge, it was actually quite specific knowledge that he held. About politics and literature, he knew nothing, and when I inquired as to why, he simply said that he did not think it important enough to waste his brain on. It explained why he cared so little for manners and propriety and why he would so easily forget the names of those he met with. It was as though his brain collected information and deleted the bits it did not find important. He had some knowledge of law, but only that which would pertain to his own business and arrests.

After a few long minutes, I gave up. "I do not see what it is that you saw, Mr. Holmes," I admitted, frustrated that I had not succeeded in clearing my mind.

In truth, I knew that I should never be successful in this venture, as my mind had not once in my life been clear of thought. My mind raced constantly and flitted from one idea to the next with the speed of a humming bird. My talent would not lie in stopping the flood gates of my thoughts, but in utilizing them to weave strong theories and understanding the dizzying threads that tied evidence together.

"The way that the wood is broken is not consistent with a fall. The splinters are far too many and the violence of the break suggests that he must have been pushed into the fixture."

I knew that this could not be all that Mr. Holmes had discovered in his time observing the book shelf, so I simply nodded for him to continue.

"This does not prove that he was murdered, only that he was killed."

I raised a quizzical brow at him.

He grinned. "Murder implies forethought. Being pushed to his death does not prove that Mr. Morton was murdered. Perhaps he was in discussion with someone and they became enraged and pushed him. This killed him, but it was not premeditated.

"If you observe the pattern of the splintering, you can see that it appears as though Mr. Morton fell at an angle, which means his attacker had to have been taller than him. This officially rules out his son, though we already knew he was innocent and it rules out Ms. Morton as well."

Mr. Holmes caught my surprised expression and confirmed, "Ms. Morton has been a suspect from the moment she hired us. My first suspect is always the victim."

"That is a bleak outlook, but I am sure a useful one," I replied.

Mr. Holmes nodded. The only thing that he seemed to enjoy more than the case itself was explaining to me his findings and seeing me understand them.

"If I am Mr. Morton," I said, turning so my back was to the book shelf, "and you are my attacker," I moved Mr. Holmes so that he was standing in front of me, "there would have to be at least the same height difference between the attacker and Mr. Morton, which means that the killer must be of not so small stature."

Mr. Holmes nodded in agreement. "Exactly, Miss Elizabeth. The attacker must be at least six feet tall."

Initially, the discovery had felt like a large break in the case, but it felt insignificant now. We still had very little to go on in our investigation and the height of a possible attacker would not narrow our search by very much.

Mr. Holmes continued talking, but I drowned him out as a returned to the black case. I had placed it on the desk after opening it and I noticed black residue flaking onto the dark wood of the desk. Mr. Holme stopped talking as he saw me staring intently at the case. I quickly began to wipe the case down with my sleeve, having no other loose fabric nearby. The black finish came off easily as I put pressure on it, revealing a cheap brown leather underneath. Had Mr. Morton been holding this piece of luggage, his fingers would have rubbed the black finish off easily. His hands had been clean on the journey and there were no markings on this case to indicate that someone had been gripping it as tightly as Mr. Morton had been.

"This is not the same case as the one Mr. Morton held on the train," I said, still removing the black finish from the case.

"How do you know that the case was not simply finished by Mr. Morton to appear finer than it was in reality?"

I ignored the question. I had been so preoccupied with the idea of seeing what was inside the case that I had not thoroughly inspected the lettering on the outside. At first glance, it looked just as I remembered, but with a closer look, it was clearly not the same. The font was similar, but each letter extended slightly too far. Its coloring was not so impressive as I remembered; the gold of the lettering on the carriage was brighter and more vibrant, than this dingy replica.

"Someone has replaced Mr. Morton's case with a counterfeit one," I said with confidence.

Mr. Holmes and I reopened the case and looked inside once more, tearing out the lining to reveal the true inside of the case, which was clearly cheaply made. Someone had taken an old case and gone through a lot of trouble to make it appear like Mr. Morton's. The question was: why?

# CHAPTER SIX:
## A Balancing Act

I continued to struggle with my time at Jane's and Mr. Bingley's home. They had been kind enough to extend my stay almost indefinitely. The pair adored having me with them, especially as the pregnancy began to affect Jane in more negative ways. She had been put to bed rest by the doctor for a week's time and I desperately wished I could remain by her side, but she insisted that she was fine. Mr. Bingley had never been more concerned and attentive with Jane. She felt that the doctor was making much too large a deal of just a small amount of sickness that came along with being with child. I felt guilt every moment I was away from her, but she would not allow it.

Mama had threatened to come visit once she heard the news that Jane was expecting. Jane had fended her off, saying that she could not handle more than one visitor at a time for now and that Mama should remain at home so to keep poor Papa and Mary company. Lydia and Kitty had left with our aunt and uncle not long after my own departure. According to Mama, they were having a nice, quiet trip thus far with little to no excitement, just as they hoped. They were all ecstatic with the news of Jane's pregnancy, of course, and each wanted to pay a visit.

Jane had been kind enough to not mention that I was being paid to work with Mr. Holmes as a detective. Mama would be horrified at the very mention of it and demand my return home at once. I had a feeling that this was also the reason Jane had refused Mama's visit. She was always thinking of me. There may not be a better sister than Jane, or a worse sister than myself.

Despite my guilt, my desire to solve Ms. Morton's case was far greater and I continued to work with Mr. Holmes. We had received a response from Sir Howard, though not in the manner we expected. Upon hearing the news of Mr. Morton's death, the man traveled to London immediately.

Apparently, Mr. Morton had saved Sir Howard's life in the war and he felt he owed him a great debt for it.

When Mr. Morton had left him, he seemed more at peace than he ever had before, as though a great weight had been lifted from his shoulders. He revealed that Mr. Morton had stayed with him for a time after the war, but he had not been in contact with him since then and that it had been a surprise that Mr. Morton wanted to come and stay with him again. Mr. Holmes and I were certain that Mr. Morton had hidden something within Sir Howard's estate and had gone to retrieve it at last, only to be killed upon his return.

When we met with Sir Howard, I first noticed his height. He was far taller than I and even slightly taller than Mr. Holmes, which made him the perfect height to have been the man who pushed Mr. Morton to his death. I knew that Mr. Holmes was of the same mind as we observed the man when he entered 221B Baker Street.

Mr. Holmes had changed the layout of his apartment to accommodate for me sitting in on his meetings with clients. Although Ms. Morton's case was our primary focus, there was no shortage of people who desired our assistance. It became clear early on that it would not continue to be effective for me to sit on the couch that was meant for clients. It put them on edge to be seated near someone they did not know nor expected to be there. We had placed another chair next to Mr. Holmes' own for me to be seated when meeting clients. It was here that I sat when Sir Howard entered the apartment.

"Am I to assume that you are Elizabeth Bennet, the young woman who wrote me that letter?" he asked. He had a warm presence that was unexpected with his stature and serious facial expression.

"I am," I said, smiling and rising from the seat to greet the gentleman.

I had become accustomed to the handshake, though I knew it to be a more improper form of greeting. I stuck out my hand for Sir Howard to take. His face was colored with confusion, but he took my hand despite this. I quickly curtsied when he took it in an effort to save the now uncomfortable greeting. Sir Howard bowed in response and kissed the top of my hand gently to assuage any awkward feelings.

"It is a pleasure to make your acquaintance, although I do wish it were under different circumstances," he said, giving a small bow in Mr. Holmes' direction.

He, of course, had neglected to stand and greet our guest. I knew Mr. Holmes' nature, so it did not come as a surprise to me, but I did think that his clients would be more at ease and willing to speak with him should he demonstrate some manners.

"As do I, Sir Howard. Mr. Morton must have been a dear friend for you to have traveled all the way out here."

He nodded, taking the seat to which I gestured. I sat down, as well.

"I owed Mr. Morton my life. He took a bullet for me on the battle front, pushed me out of the way and got hit in the leg. He nearly had to have the leg amputated and walked with a limp the rest of his life," Sir Howard said.

"Is this why you allowed Mr. Morton to stay with you directly following your return from the war?" Mr. Holmes asked.

He was not interested in any kind of pleasantries at this point. He was becoming bothered that he had not been able to figure out the case yet and his manner was reflecting that frustration. Mr. Holmes was interested in answers, as was I. I was not as frustrated with the slow process of the investigation as Mr. Holmes, but for Ms. Morton's sake, I wanted to solve it quicker than we were making progress. Sir Howard did not seem surprised by the line of questioning.

"Yes. He came from a poor family and although he should have returned hailed as a war hero, he was not, and had very little to come home to. Mr. Morton had no access to medical care, and as his injury took place while saving my life, I felt indebted to the man and allowed him to stay with me until he was healed.

"I heard how well he did once he returned to London, building his mill from the ground up and becoming a wealthy man. I wish that he had stayed in better contact over the years, but, in truth, I had not heard from him until he requested he come stay with me just recently.

"I knew the war had changed him. Even when his leg was healing, he thought there were people after him. More than one man fared similarly after the horrors of battle. When he first arrived, he seemed like an utter and complete madman. He raved about a man that had been following him, that he had found him and wanted to kill not only him but his entire family, as well. It was the same kind of story he told after the war.

"Just a few days later, his attitude shifted completely, as though nothing had bothered him in years. He enjoyed the remaining time he had at my estate before his children begged for him to return home."

It seemed as though Mr. Morton's paranoia-filled letters had been sent at the beginning of his trip if we were to take Sir Howard's word for it. Oddly, Mr. Morton did not date any of his letters, which made it difficult to create an accurate timeline of events for when he was away.

"I actually traveled into London on the same post chaise as Mr. Morton. He did not seem at ease to me. In fact, he appeared to be quite on edge," I replied. I was unsure what to make of Sir Howard's version of events.

"Yes, he did seem to become nervous as he readied himself to return to London. I thought it was just because the man who he thought had been hunting him found him when he was in London. My assumption was that he felt nervous to be returning and the feelings of paranoia was resurfacing. I tried to convince him to stay with me for a longer while, but he was adamant that he return to the city."

Mr. Holmes was sitting back in his chair, listening intently to what Sir Howard was saying. I could tell that we both felt that there were missing details in the story.

"Do you recall the luggage that Mr. Morton had with him when he arrived?" I queried.

Sir Howard did not appear surprised by the question, which bothered me. As far as Sir Howard knew, Mr. Morton's luggage had no bearing on the investigation at all and most would be taken aback by such an odd line of inquiry. My gut told me that Sir Howard either had information that would lead us to Mr. Morton's killer or he was Mr. Morton's killer. In any case, he had rehearsed his story, that was clear, and he was a skilled enough speaker that he could handle changes to his story with grace.

"He only had one case with him, which I remember thinking was odd. It was a black circular case with his name printed in gold lettering on it."

"Do you know what was held in the case?"

Sir Howard shook his head. "I never saw him open it and never thought to look inside of my friend's property, so I did not know what was inside the case when he arrived."

Mr. Holmes perked up in his seat, his back straightening. "When he arrived?"

"Pardon me?" Sir Howard replied.

"You clarified that you did not know what was inside of his case when he arrived. This implies that you know what was in the case when he left. What did Mr. Morton come to visit you for, in truth?" Mr. Holmes asked.

I knew he felt on top of his game at this moment. He had told me that if you suspect that someone is lying to you, it is important to pay close attention to the details they choose to add or leave out. This is where you can catch them in their lie. It was exactly this methodology that Mr. Holmes had used to catch Sir Howard.

"I do not know what was in the case when he arrived nor when he left. I assumed it to be one in the same," Sir Howard replied. He had managed to regain his smooth persona by the end of his rebuttal, but it was clear that he had caught his own error and was attempting to regain some of his validity.

"Whatever was inside of that case meant a lot to Mr. Morton. He held it so tightly to his chest that I feared he may break a rib on it. Whoever killed him replaced the case with a counterfeit one and wanted desperately for no one to figure it out. If you know what Mr. Morton had in his case when he left, I should think it in your best interest to share that knowledge with us, sir."

I had not intended the speech to be as venomous as it turned out, but it was just as well. Sir Howard seemed taken aback, and even Mr. Holmes seemed surprised by my thinly veiled threat. The truth was that I had no inkling as to what I was threatening Sir Howard with, only that I knew he had been hiding something from us that would enable us to protect Ms. Morton and bring her father's killer to justice.

"I did not realize what he had taken until well after his departure. I am a man of opulent taste, which I do recognize about myself. I have traveled far across the world and back, and in my travels, I purchase things that I find mysterious and beautiful. With all that I own, it did not dawn on me that I was missing anything for some time, and it was not I who noticed the missing item, but my head maid. She discovered that my most prized possession was missing. I trust all my servants with my life, and Mr. Morton had been the only new visitor for quite some time, which led me to conclude that he had stolen from me."

"What was this prized possession that Mr. Morton took from your home?" Mr. Holmes asked, clearly annoyed that Sir Howard was being so mysterious.

"A jeweled diadem," Sir Howard answered. "It was given to me in India upon our victory in the Third Carnatic War. It belonged to a princess of India. With her downfall at the hands of the powerful English militia, it was given to me as a token of our heroism and victory."

It was not lost on me how carefully Sir Howard had chosen his words in recalling how he came to own the diadem. I had the feeling that Sir Howard was not the rightful owner of the crown any more than Mr. Morton.

"When you discovered Mr. Morton had taken the diadem, were you not angry? Did you not come to London demanding that your prized possession be returned to you and when he disagreed, did you not push him, causing his death?" Mr. Holmes accused Sir Howard sharply.

"Absolutely not! I take great offense at the accusation," Sir Howard exclaimed, standing. "I was not aware that the piece was even missing until after the man was dead. Had I known before his death, I may have killed him myself."

The anger in Sir Howard's statement did not leave me questioning its truth.

"I should hope that in your investigation you shall discover where my missing diadem is and return it to me at once," Sir Howard demanded as he stormed to the door.

I forced a smile. "I assure you, Sir Howard, should the diadem be recovered, it will be returned to its rightful owner at once."

With a final dark look, he tore the door open and stomped from Mr. Holmes' apartment. I exchanged a glance with Mr. Holmes. Sir Howard was not the rightful owner of the diadem, I was sure of it, and I had no intention of returning it to him. As soon as I had this thought, I realized that Sir Howard was responsible for part of the crime.

"He was the author of the threatening note, I am sure of it."

"I could not agree with you more," Mr. Holmes said in response. "He knew about Mr. Morton's death a lot sooner than he admitted. I believe he has been in London for nearly as long as you have. He would have discovered the missing diadem much sooner if it were really his prized possession. I would safely assume that it took maybe a day before he realized it was missing and put the evidence pointing to Mr. Morton together. He left for London not long after and planned to confront

Mr. Morton, but he arrived too late and the man was already dead.

"Since he could no longer go directly to the thief, he went for Ms. Morton. Mr. Morton had stayed with him for a decent amount of time and he trusted the man. It stands to reason that he shared intimate details of his life with him, such as Ms. Morton running the business although her brother pretended to. He could not find the diadem or confront Mr. Morton about it with him being dead, and assumed that Ms. Morton would know its location."

Mr. Holmes paused and I finished his train of thought: "Sir Howard used his knowledge of Mr. Morton's paranoia to threaten Ms. Morton and hoped that her father had confided its location to her. Why would Mr. Morton steal the diadem in the first place, though? He was not for want of money from selling it and it appears as though it has gone missing."

"I think that Mr. Morton was returning the diadem to its rightful owner. Something terrible happened when they were in India and Sir Howard was commended for it with the gift of the diadem. If Mr. Morton's paranoia was not unfounded all these years, I would believe that he was being followed by the original owners of the diadem and these were the people who threatened him.

"He must have fared well enough for a while, but as his health was failing and his daughter took over the business, he began to worry about their well-being, believing that if he was not around to protect them, the rightful owners of the diadem would turn their vengeance onto his children. Not to mention, he must have feared that the events that took place in India would become public knowledge."

Mr. Holmes mused on what could have occurred in India that was so terrible, but I had stopped listening. Should our theory ring true, it was more than likely that the original owners were once again in possession of the diadem, but had killed Mr. Morton in the process of retrieving it.

# CHAPTER SEVEN:

## The Missing Treasure

We went to Ms. Morton almost immediately after our discussion with Sir Howard. The answers to our investigation were closer than ever before. Talking with Sir Howard was the break we needed in our search for the truth. We knew we were getting closer to who killed Mr. Morton and why.

When we arrived, Ms. Morton appeared exhausted. Her eyes were sunken in and her skin looked dull. She had lost even more weight since the last time we had seen her. It seemed as though the fear for her life had interfered with every aspect of her well-being. Without a sense of security, she was unable to rest for fear of being attacked and it was impossible for her to focus on anything other than her own safety. It was as though her fear for her life took away her ability to actually live. I saw a similar effect in Lydia after Mr. Wickham attacked her. She had been unable to enjoy things for a long while and could not sleep out of fear—and her attacker was dead. The effect on Ms. Morton had to be even stronger, as her would-be attacker was still out there.

"Sir Howard is the one who sent me the letter?" she asked again.

Mr. Holmes and I had both explained our interview with Sir Howard, but in her exhaustion, she had a difficult time understanding what was being said to her.

"I do not understand. You say he did not kill my father?"

"We do not believe that he is responsible for your father's death, no. There are two culprits here. One killed your father and took the diadem. They left the duplicate case in his office. The other is Sir Howard, who, in his anger at your father, unable to go after him directly, threatened you with the letter," I explained once more, this time in simple terms for her to better understand.

It was a complex case, and the idea that the man who was threatening her and the man who killed her father were separate was unexpected. I was patient with her, but Mr. Holmes was frustrated in having to explain the case to Ms. Morton so many times. He had little patience for fools and though Ms. Morton was anything but a fool, he would classify her as such for not understanding the weave of the case, even acknowledging her state.

"Do you know what occurred in India that would have affected your father in such a way?" Mr. Holmes asked.

Ms. Morton shook her head slowly. "My father never spoke of the war. He used to say that the horrors of war were not for the ears of the innocent. He kept a journal, though, and in my youth, I would sneak into his study and read snippets of his writing. I was a curious child and wanted to know my father more than he would allow. I learned many things about him from reading those. He may have written about India in one of them."

She led us back to her father's study. She had not yet cleaned the study in agreement with Mr. Holmes, should we need to return to the scene of the crime and investigate once more. It was because of this that Ms. Morton stopped at the entrance to the study, indicating that she would not join us inside.

"I do hope you find what you are looking for in my father's journals. I cannot continue on in this manner for much longer. He kept his journals in the top drawer of his desk," she said, leaving us to do our work.

It did not take Mr. Holmes and I long to uncover Mr. Morton's journals. He continued his odd habit of not dating pages in his writings, which made it difficult to discover where we could find what happened in India. Mr. Holmes read far more quickly than I and finished an entire journal before I even made it halfway through the one I was reading. He picked up another and began reading, meaning that the one he read through did not contain what we were looking for. As he sped through his pages, I slowly made my way through the journal until I came across a page describing a young Indian princess and the horrors that befell her.

"Mr. Holmes, I do believe I have discovered the Indian princess to whom the diadem belonged," I said without looking up from the page.

Her name was Manisha, and she was barely a child based upon Mr. Morton's description of her. She was to inherit her father's kingdom upon his death. Mr. Morton and his fellow soldiers killed her father, but instead of bowing down to them, her army became even more fearsome in protecting her.

In the end, it was not enough and the British forces made their way into Manisha's palace. According to Mr. Morton's recount of the events, he and his men slaughtered them all without mercy or discretion. At last, only Manisha, her mother, and their royal guard were left. Manisha's mother begged for mercy, but none was awarded them. Sir Howard ordered them to kill the girl and her mother, but to spare the guard so that he might live with his failure to protect those he swore his life to.

I read the portion aloud to Mr. Holmes, but could hardly continue. The horror of the cruelty that Sir Howard ordered upon these innocent people was too great.

In the next passage, Mr. Morton described how Sir Howard was awarded the diadem that once sat upon Manisha's head and how he treasured it as his greatest achievement.

The entire situation did not sit well with Mr. Morton and the guilt of what occurred played on his mind until his death. The guilt manifested itself in paranoia until he finally could not continue on in that manner and decided to return the diadem to its rightful owner.

Mr. Morton had been able to find Manisha's royal guard. He had been searching for him since they left him to rot amongst the bodies of his loved ones. Amrit Varma hid in shame for the rest of his life, looking for a way to find vengeance for the loss of the ones he loved. Mr. Morton gave him that path to revenge. He reached out to Mr. Varma, telling him that he knew what horrors had befallen him and that he knew the location of Manisha's diadem.

Mr. Morton paid for Mr. Varma to travel in secret to London. He was to meet with the man after he retrieved the diadem from Sir Howard's estate. Mr. Morton worked to convince Mr. Varma that killing Sir Howard would not provide him the satisfaction of revenge he wanted, but rather that stripping him of the diadem and telling the world what happened to Manisha and her people would. Mr. Morton insisted that Sir Howard would do better to have to live in shame as he forced Mr. Varma to do all those years ago.

With this information, it was not hard for Mr. Holmes and I to deduce what happened. Mr. Morton had attempted to shield his involvement in the massacre, but when Mr. Varma came to retrieve the diadem, he recognized Mr. Morton as one of the men who participated in the atrocities. In his anger, he pushed Mr. Morton, who fell to his death. Mr. Varma took the case with the diadem inside, which was the plan all along. It was Mr. Morton who made the counterfeit case so that no one would notice it missing. Mr. Varma would have to take the real case, as he needed a subtle and safe way to travel with the diadem. The real case was luxurious and had padding inside, which was perfect to keep the diadem safe on the journey back to India.

"It is likely that we have missed our window in apprehending Mr. Amrit Varma for the death of

Mr. Morton," I said to Mr. Holmes as we finished surmising.

"I am not so certain that we have," he replied. "Part of Mr. Morton's plan was to expose Sir Howard for the villain that he is. Mr. Morton was probably going to release the truth in the London news reel to tarnish Sir Howard's reputation. Mr. Varma would need to play that role now with the death of Mr. Morton." He seemed to be lost in thought for a moment. "I do not believe that Mr. Varma has left London, and I think I know where he is staying."

Mr. Holmes and I left Ms. Morton's in a hurry. Mr. Holmes claimed that Mr. Varma, being a man of higher standing and used to some degree of comfort, would be staying in a hotel. There were not many hotels in London that would cater to him, and Mr. Holmes thought he knew which one had taken the man in. It was the Hog's Head Inn that we were headed towards.

I was not so convinced. A royal guard may be used to comfort, but Mr. Amrit Varma had been shunned, living in shame for decades. He might not even be staying anywhere and could be finding shelter on the streets. Still, I agreed that should Mr. Holmes be right, it would be much simpler to see if he was, in fact, staying at the Hog's Head Inn. Mr. Holmes knew the owners there, which gave us an advantage, as he was certain they would tell him if Mr. Amrit Varma was one of their guests.

As we entered the Hog's Head Inn, it turned out that we did not even have to ask the owners if Amrit Varma was staying there. Although we did not know what he looked like, it was unlikely that there were many Indian men staying here and the man who was almost certainly Amrit Varma sat peacefully in the drawing room opposite the check-in desk.

Mr. Holmes walked up to him and asked without preface, "Are you Mr. Amrit Varma?"

"I am," Mr. Varma replied with a nod. "I am of the assumption that you are here to arrest me for Mr. Morton's death."

His calm nature was unsettling to me.

"We are not police. We have no authority to make an arrest," I responded.

Mr. Varma looked up at me with mild surprise. "But you know who I am and what I have done."

I nodded.

"Then you have told the police where to find me."

Mr. Holmes and I exchanged a glance. The truth was that we had been so preoccupied in solving the case that we had not even thought to notify Scotland Yard. The police still looked at Mr. Morton's death as an unfortunate accident.

Mr. Varma did not seem concerned with our lack of response. “I regret that I killed Mr. Morton, but he paid for his crimes with his repentance and his life. It will not be long before the story of what happened to Manisha is told. The diadem has been returned to my people. I accept that I must now pay for my crime of killing Mr. Morton.”

After that, Mr. Varma fell silent and did not speak another word to myself or Mr. Holmes.

Eventually, officers from Scotland Yard came to arrest Mr. Varma, although it took some convincing, as they were not even aware that a murder had taken place. Mr. Varma went calmly with them. He was a man at complete peace. With the knowledge that his vengeance on Sir Howard would be exacted and the diadem was once again where it belonged, he had no reason to be in anguish.

As he was being led by the officers out of the inn, he turned to myself and Mr. Holmes. “I shall live the rest of my years in peace, and I hope that death brought Mr. Morton the peace he deserved,” he said before the officers forced him through the door.

His statement could have two meanings, either that he truly hoped Mr. Morton had found peace or that he felt Mr. Morton did not deserve peace and hoped the man would suffer for eternity for his crimes. I hoped for the former.

# CHAPTER EIGHT:
## A Proposal

I was set to return to Longbourn only a week after the arrest of Mr. Varma. The news ran the story of Sir Howard's atrocities, after which he fled from London back to his estate in the country. It was rumored that the man might have his knighthood revoked should the story prove truthful. Mr. Holmes and I ensured that the evidence incriminating Sir Howard went to the right people to make it so.

With Sir Howard's focus being on feigning his innocence and hiding in the country, Ms. Morton no longer had to concern herself with his now empty threats. Although she had discovered such unsavory information about her father's past, she did not regret her decision to have Mr. Holmes and I solve her case. She was glad to know the truth and the peace of mind she had from knowing the threats against her life were now empty was worth any amount of trouble. Ms. Morton was grateful that her father's killer would be brought to justice, but she confided in me that she was not sure if it was justice in this case. She felt as though Mr. Varma had suffered enough in his time and some portion of that suffering had been due to her father's actions. I assured her that Mr. Varma himself wanted to atone for killing her father, but she still did not feel right that the man was set to remain in jail for the rest of his days. Ms. Morton would have preferred it if Sir Howard had been the one to have been imprisoned for her father's death.

Mr. Holmes had already returned to his work with new clients. We had seen a fair number of clients while still investigating Ms. Morton's case, but none of them had offered any more work than a couple hours inquiry. It took only moments for Mr. Holmes to desire a new case after we officially closed Ms. Morton's. I had a fervor for detective work, but nothing compared to Mr. Holmes' insatiable desire to work constantly. I needed time to decompress after solving the case, but Mr. Holmes could turn around at a moment's notice and begin to solve a new one. I had thought that my desire to rest after solving the case of Mr. Wickham was because it had such a great effect on my family, but I felt similarly after we solved Ms. Morton's case.

I wanted nothing more than to be by Jane's side as she grew rounder with each day. It was no longer possible for her to hide her bump, it had grown so large. The doctor lifted her bed rest, but forbade her from doing any strenuous activity, which I teased meant Mama should never be allowed to visit while Jane was with child. Jane chastised me for the jibe, but with a smile. The week following the case was just like my first week in London. The only thing that was different was that Mr. Holmes had requested my presence more than once, but I declined, wishing to remain with Jane and Mr. Bingley.

"You cannot ignore Mr. Holmes' requests to see you forever," Jane said as the maid handed me another letter from the man in question.

"I know, but I need a short reprieve from him, and do you blame me?" I asked, though I knew the answer.

I had told Jane the entire story and read the article that ousted Sir Howard's true nature to both her and Mr. Bingley. The pair of them thought it to be a ghastly thing and could hardly stand my recount of the events. I, however, found that I was as satisfied by recounting the story of the case as I was in solving it. Mr. Bingley even complimented my storytelling skills, though he thought it would be better should my subject be anything more cheerful than a murder case.

"I do not blame you, dear Lizzie, but you have been glued to Mr. Holmes' side for some time now, you cannot just stop," she scolded. "You must at least explain why you are not calling upon him now."

"I shall soon be back to myself and in want of another case to solve, but I am in desperate need of caring for my dear sister and no one else," I said, pulling her into a tight hug.

She laughed, returning my embrace. "You are far sweeter than you let anyone know, Lizzie," Jane said, brushing my hair from my face. "You may have a morbid fascination and a unique talent for solving crimes, but you use them to help those around you."

I sighed. "I worry that Mr. Holmes works as a consulting detective for far different reasons than I."

Jane looked at me with a puzzled expression. "What do you mean?"

"He seems to find life dull without the constant distraction of a mysterious tragedy. I fear that he is too reliant on the job and without it finds the world meaningless. I too like solving cases for my own selfish reasons, but I care and empathize with those affected by the cases in a way that Mr. Holmes does not seem to be capable."

"I understand why this might concern you, but Lizzie, once the sun goes down, does the reason for what you do matter so much as the fact that you do it? The pair of you have done many a good deed and helped bring justice to so many that would not have had it otherwise. Whether Mr. Holmes does it because it is the only fulfillment in his life, while a sad fact, should not change the positive outcome of your work."

Jane's words made more sense than I cared to admit. In my dissatisfaction with being proved wrong, I simply nodded in response.

"I know that you require time between cases, but do you believe that you will desire to work with Mr. Holmes once more?" Jane asked.

"I have no doubt in my mind that I shall," I responded. "I can already feel in the back of my mind the desire to return to 221B Baker Street to piece together another puzzle."

"Charles and I spoke not long ago, and you know that you are welcome to stay here as long as you like." Jane paused. "You planned to leave for Longbourn at the end of this week, correct?"

I nodded in agreement, wondering what Jane was trying to say. "That is the plan as it stands now."

"Charles and I thought it might be useful for you to be around until a little after the baby comes, if not longer. The doctor has relieved me of bed rest, but still does not want me to do much on my own and I would so prefer having you here to help me than anyone else."

My heart leapt at the idea of being able to remain in London for such a long while. I wanted desperately to aid Jane in any way that I could and I was gleeful at the thought of remaining in the city long enough to see her child born. It was not hard to deduce her ulterior motives for extending this invitation to me. She was telling the truth in that it would greatly relieve her duties should I remain, but she had left out that she wanted me to be able to continue my work with Mr. Holmes.

Jane was far more accepting than I expected her to be of my desire to be an old maid that lived off of her own income. I suspected that she hoped Mr. Holmes and I would become romantic partners in the future, though I knew that would never be the case. I thanked her a thousand times over for her invitation to remain in London with her and Mr. Bingley and left her at once to write to Mama and tell her the news. She was sure to insist upon visiting now, which would actually be quite nice for Jane. It might be difficult for me to explain to her what I was doing with Mr. Holmes and that I was making my own income, but I had a feeling deep in my gut that Mama would accept it eventually.

Not one day later did I return to 221B Baker Street.

Without the dread of returning home, I realized that though I required some time after cases, part of my reason for distancing myself from Mr. Holmes was that I did not want to leave. I distanced myself in order to make the farewell to both Mr. Holmes and our work less painful, though it would not have been successful in doing so.

Mrs. Hudson answered the door. She was delighted to see me.

"I thought that you were meant to be returning home soon?" she inquired after letting me into the building.

"I was slated to leave in just a couple days, but my sister requested that I extend my stay. With the babe coming, she is not meant to be doing much around the house, and my presence will make it easier on Jane."

Mrs. Hudson smiled at me. "What a dear sister you are," she said, her cheeks rosy and round as ever. "I expect that you shall stay for tea before you leave."

"I shall do just that, Mrs. Hudson," I replied before heading up the stairs to Mr. Holmes' apartment. It was quiet inside, so I did not wait long before knocking and entering.

"Miss Elizabeth," Mr. Holmes said as I entered the room. "I confess I did not expect you to return."

"I am sorry for that, Mr. Holmes. Jane needed me by her side for a time and I must confess that I needed time between the end of Ms. Morton's case and the start of a new one."

Mr. Holmes nodded, though I saw his brow scrunch up when I mentioned the beginning of a new case.

"I suppose that you have come to bid your farewells," he said cooly. He had remained in his chair and kept his nose in a book the entire time I had been in the room. My chair remained beside his, though I chose to take the seat across from him. "Farewell."

I almost laughed at his attempt at a nonchalant goodbye. "Actually, I am here for an entirely different reason."

Mr. Holmes finally peered up at me from his book. "What reason might that be?" he asked.

"Jane has requested that I remain in London until after her child is born."

Mr. Holmes perked up at this, raising his head fully from the book.

"I have to help her around the house," I continued, "but I expect that I shall have a fair amount of time to spare. I hoped that you might be interested in having me continue as your associate consulting detective." I ended my request with a grin, knowing full well what his answer would be.

"I suppose that can be arranged," he responded with a smile, closing the book that he had been pretending to read.

"Shall I share with you the details of our next case?" he asked, to which I replied an enthusiastic yes.

FROM THE JANE AUSTEN NOVEL
*Pride & Prejudice*

# THE PECULIAR DOCTOR BARNABUS

*A Sherlock Holmes & Elizabeth Bennet Mystery*

AMELIA LITTLEWOOD

CYANIDE PUBLISHING

# CHAPTER ONE:

## Caring and Concern

It had not dawned on me that working with Mr. Holmes could be dangerous. I do not know why the thought had not crossed my mind. Perhaps the excitement held me in its grasp so tightly that the danger became no more than an afterthought. I had not entertained the notion that solving crimes might one day put me in danger, but Mr. Bingley and Jane voiced their concern for me unrelentingly. Though I wanted to heed their concerns, I could not help but feel that they were unwarranted. Mr. Holmes and I had not had any new cases for a long while. It had put both of us in foul moods. I do not like to admit that my countenance was so dependent on my work with Mr. Holmes, but I found that I was at my happiest when I was working with him to solve a case. My mind felt like it had no occupation otherwise.

"Lizzie, could you be a dear and pass that to me?" Jane said from the other side of the drawing room.

She was resting on the ornate velvet couch, her hand laying on top of her ever-growing pregnant stomach. The physician had told Jane and Mr. Bingley that she should remain as immobile as possible, much to Jane's discomfort. She had no interest or desire to remain seated at all times, unhelpful and bored. Jane had done well thus far, and remained dutifully in bed or seated when Mr. Bingley was around, but flitted about the house as usual when he was not. This, she told me, was the key to a happy marriage. To me it felt almost deceitful, which I applauded coming from Jane, as she had never so much as harmed a fly. She maintained that she simply did not want Mr. Bingley to worry about her, and that she would be fine.

I trained my eyes to where she was pointing. A small diary that she wrote in rested on the fine oak table by the end of the couch.

"Of course," I replied, standing from my perch and walking towards the table. The room felt uncomfortably warm for the time of year, adding to the slow, lazy feeling of the day. I had been seated on the large bench underneath the window for so long that my legs had become tingly with disuse. I was deeply immersed in the book I was reading, not because it was particularly good, but simply because it was something to occupy me for the time being. I had not actually registered Jane's request for a few moments and she had sat expectantly waiting for my response.

"Are you alright?" she asked, concerned.

I nodded and smiled at her, hoping to be reassuring as I handed her the book. Jane liked to read over what she had written, and so didn't request any writing implement to add a new entry.

"I am quite alright," I said, unable to hide my dissatisfaction with how the day had gone. I had been waiting for Mr. Holmes to call for the better part of the morning. If he did not soon, then I would know that he was once again refusing to meet with potential clients. Jane, knowing me better than I do myself, did not ask again or push to ask why I felt upset. She and I knew that I would not want to speak out loud what was bothering me.

Mr. Holmes had been recluse for a fortnight. He refused to answer when I called upon him, Mrs. Hudson apologizing to me as I stood dumbly at the base of the stairs. Though Mr. Holmes had not shared his demons with me, I was not blind to them. I knew he suffered extensively when the cases dried up, far more than I did. He was not one to handle boredom well, and appeared to drown in long bouts of depression and melancholy. It was this that kept him from wanting to see me.

It was not that there was a lack of clients or cases to investigate, but they were all rather simple cases, each solved in a short amount of time. Many Mr. Holmes was miraculously able to solve before the clients even completed their explanations of the cases. I could never cease to be amazed by his capabilities. There truly was no match to his wit, and I doubt there ever shall be. His genius was his curse as much as it was his gift.

"Miss Bennet, there's a letter for you. It's just arrived," said the kindly maid, coming into the drawing room.

Jane raised slightly, still unused to her new last name and standing as a married woman. For a moment, she thought that it was she who was being addressed. Still standing, I graciously took the letter from the maid. Jane smiled warmly at the woman before she quietly excused herself. I knew immediately that the letter would be from Mr. Holmes. My heart leapt as I took in his handwriting on the outside that confirmed my suspicions.

"It's from Mr. Holmes, isn't it?" Jane asked, concern once again coloring her voice.

When I was bored without work from him she was concerned, but she was just as concerned when I was working with him.

"It is," I replied.

Her lips twitched disapprovingly, but she did not say anything more. I ignored her disapproval and tore the letter open. As I had hoped, he was requesting I visit his apartment at 221B Baker Street. He claimed that there were a few potential clients that had piqued his interest and he required my presence in order to interview them.

I sprang into action and headed from the drawing room with a quick goodbye to Jane, who waved pleasantly. I was always amazed by how her demeanor changed so easily. Though she was concerned for my safety, she was pleased to see me happy and thus allowed me to leave without trouble.

"Lizzie, may I speak with you for a moment?" Mr. Bingley's voice called from his study at the rear of the house.

I stopped mid-step and turned towards the study. It was not often that Mr. Bingley requested an audience with me alone and it was rarer still for him to call me Lizzie. Typically, he still referred to me by my full name or as Miss Bennet. Always a gentleman, he was a slave to propriety and had not gotten used to my more casual address.

"Absolutely," I replied loudly enough that Mr. Bingley would hear me as I went towards his study. I peered in, feeling as though I was intruding even though he had invited me inside moments ago.

"Ah, Lizzie, how are you?" he asked pleasantly. His and Jane's demeanors were so complimentary to one another, endlessly kind.

"I'm well. Just on my way out, actually," I replied.

My excitement to meet with Mr. Holmes and potentially get a new case precluded my manners. Mr. Bingley just smiled broadly at me, but there was clearly something that he wanted to speak with me about. His eyes betrayed his true seriousness.

"Off to see Mr. Holmes?" He asked, the skepticism in his voice further betrayed the subject that he wanted to speak with me about.

My heart began to sink for a moment. I could only work with Mr. Holmes for as long as Mr. Bingley's and Jane's generosity remained, and though I knew it to be endless, the less logical part of me thought anxiously of them turning me out. I did not answer quickly enough, so Mr. Bingley continued on without my answer. Regardless of my answering or not, we both knew what I would have replied with.

"I am concerned for Jane's wellbeing."

This was not what I had expected and took me by surprise. I had become so used to him and

Jane voicing their concern for me that I had not expected he would be concerned for Jane, as well.

"Because of the pregnancy?" I queried. "She has been resting a fair amount, I'm sure she and the babe are more than alright."

Mr. Bingley smiled at me once more, but I could see the concern clearly painted on his face. He was a young man, but the worry creased his face, making him look older than he was. "She has been complaining of pains. Some have been so severe that she loses the ability to move and even to speak."

Jane had hidden this well from me thus far. I had no inkling that my dear sister had been in any pain at all. The idea of Jane in such pain hurt me to my very core and it was clear on Mr. Bingley's face that it pained him as well.

"I did not know. Jane never said." I sank into the seat near Mr. Bingley's desk.

"No, she didn't want you to know, but I feel as though you should." He did look mildly conflicted by making this decision for her, when she expressly stated that she desired opposite to what he was doing. "The doctor says that these spasms of pain are a result of stress."

"Is that why she has been recommended to remain in bed or as stationary as manageable?"

Mr. Bingley nodded.

I was grateful that he had chosen to tell me about dear Jane's pain, but I knew he had more to say. There had to be a more compelling reason for him to betray Jane's trust so explicitly.

"I… I do believe that it is possible you are the cause of this stress," he said uncomfortably.

I was immediately insulted by this assumption, my hand jumping to my heart. I had no knowledge that my presence had become stressful for either Jane or Mr. Bingley, though neither would typically give me reason to think so.

Mr. Bingley quickly lifted his hands in defense, with his palms up. "I don't mean to offend, and it is not your being here that is stressful, but Jane is terribly concerned for your safety. She worries endlessly that you will be harmed on one of your adventures with Mr. Holmes."

I could see that Mr. Bingley felt terribly uncomfortable speaking with me about this and I felt equally uncomfortable with the conversation.

"I did not know," I said, unsure of what else to say.

Mr. Bingley nodded and there was an awkward moment of silence between the two of us. I knew that for this conversation to go the way the Mr. Bingley hoped I would immediately agree to end my investigations with Mr. Holmes. Both he and I knew that this would surely never be the case.

"I am sorry and shall attempt to be more careful," I finally managed.

"Please do, Lizzie. It would be the end of our dear Jane should anything happen to you."

I left in a sullen mood. I always had a propensity for selfishness and had not even seriously considered how my actions affected those closest to me. I could feel the guilt of my conversation with Mr. Bingley weighing on me already as I exited the grand home. Mr. Bingley had not been trying to make me feel guilty. He was far too kind to purposefully make anyone feel negatively. Truthfully, the guilt I had felt was not due to Mr. Bingley's statements. I had been resisting the feelings for quite some time. I knew the only reason that they permitted my odd relationship and work with Mr. Holmes was because it made me happy, and my dear father's reasons for allowing it were the same. Other than my happiness they did not understand the importance of the work I did, and in many ways condemned it.

I was consumed by these thoughts my entire journey to Mr. Holmes' apartment. It was ironic that these thoughts were all that occupied my mind, but I still made my way to Baker Street, my selfish nature already overtaking the care I should have had for my loved ones. The excitement I had when Mr. Holmes first contacted me resurfaced as the carriage arrived outside of his apartment door. I knew that he must have been contacted by a very promising client to drag him out of his dark mood.

"Lizzie, dear, I've been expecting you!" Mrs. Hudson greeted me kindly, answering the door before I had even gotten the chance to knock on it. I startled slightly, not expecting such a swift greeting.

"Hello, Mrs. Hudson. How are you?" I asked, genuinely interested.

I had begun to think of Mrs. Hudson as a dear friend of mine and loved to hear her stories, of which she had plenty. After hearing one such story, I remained seated with her longer than I would normally. I could hear Mr. Holmes pacing above us.

Leaning in towards Ms. Hudson, I whispered, "How is he?"

She did not have to answer, her face giving away that Mr. Holmes had not been well at all.

"He's been much like how he was before," she said ominously.

She did not offer any further explanation, but I think I knew what she meant. I sighed, and sensing that it was beyond time for me to go to Mr. Holmes, I excused myself and made the way up the stairs to his apartment.

# CHAPTER TWO:

## The Scarred Beggar

"Lizzie, nice of you to *finally* join me," Mr. Holmes said with sarcasm.

His eyes were wide and wild. I could see the disarray of the past fortnight plainly in his appearance and in his apartment. Though Mr. Holmes often appeared disheveled, his appearance now was unlike any I had seen previously. He was dressed in a suit, but in place of a jacket he wore his dressing gown. His tie was askew and his hair looked as though he had not run a comb through it in many days. It was not only his appearance that gave him such a wild look, but the sheen of slight insanity in his eyes that lent to this feeling of disorganized energy. The apartment itself was in complete disarray and smelled dreadful. Mr. Holmes did not rise to greet me, but had yelled through the door for me to enter.

"Glad to see you, Mr. Holmes," I replied, bringing my hand up to cover my nose, the smell of the rotting food in his kitchen overwhelming me.

I had not been used to such a lifestyle as Mr. Holmes'. Though my childhood was peppered with concern for mine and my sisters' futures, we grew up well and comfortably. We never wanted for anything and servants cared for things such as cooking and cleaning, Mr. Holmes did not live this way. Though we worked for good money and he clearly came from a wealthier background than I, his home was always in a state of complete disarray. Mrs. Hudson would often run about the apartment tidying as best she could, but Mr. Holmes seemed to do nothing to better his state of living. Knowing that he chose to live in this manner always perplexed me. Should I ever live alone, without any assistance, I would hope that I would care more for my environment.

"Our client should be here momentarily," he said, ignoring my reaction to the state of his home.

I had to muffle a few coughs that I could not fully suppress. I finally located the source of the smell, an old plate of food resting on the kitchen table that I believed Mr. Holmes had not touched at all in the last fortnight.

He was seated in his chair but had not stopped moving since shouting to allow me entrance. His eyes darted around the room and it seemed as though he was unable to focus them on anything. His leg moved uncontrollably and his fingers tapped incessantly on the arm of his chair.

The apartment itself was covered in loose papers as though he had thrown them about the place. A large pile of books had toppled over and remained strewn on the floor. Mr. Holmes had clothing laying around the apartment as though he had rummaged through his closet and was unable to choose what to wear.

"And it seems promising?" I asked.

Mr. Holmes nodded. "Very promising, indeed," he replied with a sly, excited smile.

I startled as he laughed abruptly.

"Finally, Lizzie, a case!" he said, louder than necessary.

He was wild with excitement in a way I don't believe I could ever feel. I do not know if I could not achieve this excitement because I had never been allowed to feel such intensity of emotion or because Mr. Holmes' excitement was simply such a contrast to the melancholy he had been feeling.

I looked once again at the state of the apartment, feeling as though we could not rightfully accept visitors there. Had I been a client with no knowledge of Mr. Holmes as a man, I would not hire nor even remain long enough to speak with him.

"Might I suggest cleaning before the client arrives?" I asked gently, not wanting to cause offense.

Mr. Holmes, who had been sitting restlessly in his chair, stopped his jittering leg and looked up at me. "Why would I do that?" he asked, sounding genuinely confused by my suggestion.

There was a coldness to his voice that I had not heard before. I knew that Mr. Holmes could be harder than I had witnessed. He was always softer with me than with others. I do not know why this was, but it was. Possibly it was that we were kindred spirits, both on the outskirts of a society that condemned what we desired. We had a connection that went further than any romantic relationship or otherwise, an understanding that we both wanted more that what our lot in life was meant to be. It seemed as though I would soon be privy to this darker and harsher side of him. When I first began to work with him, I had read varying accounts of him. Mr. Holmes had been commonly referred to as rude, abrupt, and unkind, none of which was what I experienced from him.

"I would not expect a client to hire us or remain in this apartment for long," I said as Mr. Holmes once again resumed jittering his leg.

"What does the state of my home have to do with my capabilities as a consulting detective?"

Mr. Holmes had gone cold once more. He seemed to prefer to be on the edge of social acceptability. Everything about his outward appearance was designed to express this to the outside world and it seemed as though this was also the case with his apartment.

"Nothing, but not many would like to spend time amid the scent of rotted sustenance and complete disarray," I replied, harsher than I intended, though I did mean it.

Mr. Holmes glared at me from his chair, a darkness creeping across his face. He looked like a storm laying in wait, ready to break at any moment. I had never been fearful of Mr. Holmes, but now I was.

"I do not mean to offend, but I do not think any client would remain for long with the state of your apartment." I tried to step back from my words. I truly did not mean to offend, though I did not think that any man in their right mind would trust in Mr. Holmes based on this first impression.

"I am not offended, though I am disappointed in you."

It was my turn to be offended in this conversation. "You are disappointed in *me*?" I asked incredulously.

He nodded.

"In what way have I disappointed you, sir?" I demanded.

"I did not think that you would be one to bother with societal expectations, as your presence here goes against all of them." As he spoke, his words became harsher and faster, betraying that I had in fact given offense with my statement.

"Truly, Mr. Holmes, I only meant that you might require a cleaner space to meet with those who actually choose to be a part of society," I replied quickly.

I did not care for how he purposefully tried to be a recluse from society, it was not something that came naturally to him, but something that he worked for. He felt himself better than everyone else and in this moment, he clearly belied that he was better than myself.

"If I did not know you, I would not stay for a moment longer than entering the door," I added. Shameful though it is to admit, I wanted to hurt his feelings as he had wounded my pride.

"I believe that you can leave, Miss Bennet, if you do not want to be here," he said darkly. I knew by his tone that it was not suggestion, but an order for me to leave.

Without another word, I left the dirty apartment. I did not know why this meeting was so contentious, but I suspect that Mr. Holmes' previous fortnight of depression did not help. I cannot claim to be innocent in this confrontation, not wholly anyways. The conversation I had had with Mr. Bingley prior to my arrival had been weighing on me, and my frustration with that had affected me in such a way that I took it out on Mr. Holmes and forgot my manners.

I had sent the carriage away, telling the driver to return to pick me up in a few hours, not expecting my stay to be cut so short. With no other recourse, I chose to take the long walk back home. The idea of having to walk home was not an unwelcome one, as I had not been allowed or able to walk great distances since I had arrived in London. I enjoyed walking and missed being able to walk aimlessly for long hours in the country. In the city, everyone who was walking was walking to something. In the country, you did not have to walk somewhere specific, but in the city, it seemed as though it was almost not allowed to be walking without a specific place in mind to wind up. I appreciated the time the walk home would give me to think about the interactions I had with both Mr. Holmes and Mr. Bingley. Both conversations were equally troubling, albeit for different reasons.

The brisk air hit me as I left the apartment. Mrs. Hudson had tried to stop me to have another chat, but I had not been in the mood and quickly got myself out of the conversation. I stumbled into the street and immediately bumped into a man in tattered clothing. He smelled worse than the apartment I had just left. I managed to refrain from covering my nose this time, more concerned with offending this man than I had been with Mr. Holmes.

"I am sorry, sir. I did not see you," I said.

The man glanced up at me. A large scar covered the entire left side of his face. It was a nasty thing, red and irritated as if it was not very old, though it appeared entirely healed. It went through his eye, causing it to remain shut. The hair in his eyebrows and lashes were gone where the scar tissue had grown.

"I tend to be rather unseeable," he replied with a toothy grin.

His teeth were immaculately white and straight, not at all what one would expect from a beggar. I smiled at him uncomfortably and began to walk away. I found the man very unsettling and wanted to be away from him as quickly as possible. As I passed, his hand slithered out from his coat and he grabbed my arm. I pulled it away from him and turned to him.

"Excuse me, sir," I said, startled by the action.

His hand was outstretched toward me as though he was asking for money. Sighing, I reached into my purse and passed a few small coins to him. He gripped them tightly. To avoid having to interact with the man any more I turned and briskly walked from him. I knew that had Jane or Mr. Bingley been the ones to bump into the man, they would have given far more than I, but I could not help feeling deeply unsettled by the scarred man and had shoved whatever coins were at the top of my purse into his hand.

I had only walked a few more feet when I realized that the scent of the beggar had not left me. It did not take much for me to realize that the man was trailing behind me. He was not being very subtle about following me. His stench was more than enough to give him away, but even more than that, he was close enough behind me that I could hear his footsteps and see the swish of his brown coat in my peripheral vision. I thought momentarily that he might simply be going in the same direction as I, but it was clear that he had been walking in the opposite direction when we collided with one another.

"Sir, are you following me?" I asked him as I turned, deciding that it was better to confront him rather than ignore his presence.

"Are you in league with Mr. Holmes?" he asked.

I had not noticed that his accent was one of affluence. His word choice was odd. I supposed that I was in league with Mr. Holmes, though that was not the way that I would have worded it.

"How do you know that?" I asked. The thought of denying it did not even cross my mind, though that would have been more sensible.

"I am interested in the services you provide."

"Then you will have to set up an appointment to speak with Mr. Holmes," I said.

The scarred man had completely thrown me. I was unsure how he knew that I worked with Mr. Holmes or why he was approaching me on the street instead of scheduling a formal meeting.

"Good day," I said with as much finality as I could muster and continued on my journey home.

"How would I procure one of these appointments, Miss Elizabeth?"

I stopped mid-step as he said my name. My eyes narrowed as I turned back to him.

"How do you know my name?"

Suspicion was gnawing at the pit of my stomach. I felt bile was rising in my throat. I had never had such an intense confrontation with such a strange man. For all my confidence, I truly had no knowledge of the world. I had lived a sheltered country life and was not used to the hardness of the city. I knew that Jane was much affected by the pain and hardship she saw everyday outside the windows of her grand estate. Were it up to her, all her and Mr. Bingley's wealth would go to the poor and needy.

"I know many things, and I tend to go quite unnoticed," he replied, giving me another grin. It felt like less like a smile and more like a threat.

"You can contact Mr. Holmes about meeting with him, though it is quite costly."

I hoped that this would be enough to end the conversation, but it did not seem like I would be able to any time soon. His entire presence felt oily to me, his face was slick with it. His dark black hair was mostly covered by a brown bowler hat with fraying edges, but I could see that his hair was tight to his scalp. This was not because it was cut short or lacked in length—the opposite was true in fact—but because it was greased back as though it was wet. He stood close to me and I felt claustrophobic at his closeness. I could feel my heart beat in my throat as I finished my statement. His expression darkened similarly to how Mr. Holmes' had when I offended him. I wished for Mr. Holmes to be here as I became more and more unsettled by the scarred man.

"I can handle the cost," he said darkly as he forced the coins I had given him back into my hand roughly.

I gasped at the violence of his motion, not expecting such a reaction. He stalked off, pushing past me. His shoulder collided with mine and his stench was overwhelming as he breezed by me. I gagged once and quickly regained composure. There were more than one set of curious eyes on me and though I was relatively anonymous, should anyone recognize me, word could get back to Mr. Bingley and Jane. I did not like feeling as though I had to keep things from either of them, but Mr Bingley's words echoed in my mind. I knew that if Jane were to find out about such an odd interaction, she would be worried. Normally this would not matter, but now I knew that Jane’s health was directly affected by my actions with Mr. Holmes.

# CHAPTER THREE:

## The Ring Leader

I was able to make it home without further incident following my encounter with the scarred beggar man. It was true that I had begun to think of Jane and Mr. Bingley's estate as home. It was a bittersweet realization that a new place could become home so easily. I do not know if the effect of working with Mr. Holmes was what made London feel like home, but I had felt more like myself than I ever had before, so much so that this sensation may have altered my view of London so it felt more like home than home ever had.

I admit that I felt somewhat sad to realize that I had come to think of a place other than Longbourn as home. But should that not be as it was naturally? If I were to be married, I would have had to make a new place my home and I would rarely have the opportunity to see Longbourn again. I would have been occupied with the business of running my own household. Although I was going about things in an alternate manner, my choosing a new place as home in my new occupation as a true adult was only fitting and natural.

To my surprise, I was greeted by Mr. Bingley the moment I walked through the front door. He looked rather serious and my heart leapt into my throat, my thoughts immediately going to Jane. Could something have happened to her?

Something of my fear must have shown in my expression, for Mr. Bingley halted and his face gentled. "Oh, Elizabeth, I fear that I've made you worried beyond what you should be."

"I admit that the manner of your approach made me fear for our Jane."

Mr. Bingley shook his head. "She is a bit concerned, but her health is quite well today."

"She is concerned? Has there been distressing news?"

Mr. Bingley's face turned thoughtful. "It has been decided that we should invite your younger sisters to visit us. Jane has had news from your mother that the three of them at Longbourn are quite tired of one another's company, if we may be frank about the matter, and that Mary would rather benefit from some travel."

I rather agreed on that account. Mary was very withdrawn and shy and only showed herself when performing on the pianoforte or quoting a book she had read. She considered herself quite accomplished and learned, and I feared she did not realize what a sheltered life she had led. Not to say that my life had not been sheltered in its own way, but Mary had no friends, disliked the balls, and had yet to travel. I worried that she had little not only in the way of understanding the world but of understanding people and would be left quite alone once our parents were gone. Whether through marriage or friendship or some other means, I hoped that she would learn to interact with those around her and find her place in society.

"It was also expressed that we should invite Kitty and Lydia along," Mr. Bingley continued. "We all felt it would benefit them to properly enter society and take advantage of the many things London has to offer by way of culture and people."

For Lydia and Kitty, I held more concern in coming to London, but for very different reasons.

Lydia was still much changed after her encounter with Mr. Wickham. His attack upon her had been vile and had quite altered her character. I hoped that her trip with Kitty had done her good, but I feared that London would prove a frightening place for her. In our country towns we mingled with those of the same social class which, on its own, I had found to be narrow-minded. But it also afforded protection from seeing the darker sides of society. In my time in London I had seen homeless men and desperate women and all manner of drunkards. London might yet prove too much for Lydia.

Kitty, on the other hand, might be altogether too dazzled by it. She had supplanted Lydia as the liveliest one among us, although her intentions were mainly to try and raise Lydia's spirits, for which I could little blame her. The two youngest girls were near inseparable, just as Jane and I were. As Lydia grew quiet, Kitty grew loud to counter-balance her. But Kitty, although aware of what had nearly befallen Lydia, was still in that innocent daze of feeling that it couldn't possibly happen to her, and I was greatly concerned that she might get herself into trouble while in London.

However, I could not deny the many social advantages that being in London would entail. Mr. Bingley was well-connected and had many great friends among the upper class. Kitty and Lydia were both close enough to marrying age that Mother would be anxious to see them acquainted with the various young gentlemen of fortune. And while I was not inclined towards marriage since my acquaintance with Mr. Holmes, it had been all that Lydia and Kitty had desired since they were children, and my choice was not theirs. Who was I to deny them what they wanted for their futures?

"I fear that their arrival may overwhelm Jane," I admitted, "but if she has decided she can handle it, I have no objection."

"Are you certain?" Mr. Bingley said. He paused for a moment and I felt as though there was something I was missing. "Does this mean you will cease to visit Mr. Holmes?"

My heart sank and I realized what he was getting at. My visits to Mr. Holmes could not be well-hid from my three sisters, all of whom were inquisitive by nature. Once they knew, my secret would not remain such for much longer, for they were sure to write back to Mother and Father. Father seemed to accept my choices even if he did not always approve of them, but Mother, I knew, would be quite upset.

Mr. Bingley must have seen the realization cross my face, for he nodded. "I urge you, Lizzie, to tell your mother what you have been doing. What you are continuing to do, if in fact you are continuing it. She deserves to know and this secret cannot continue to be such. It will hurt her far more if she hears it as gossip than if you tell her yourself."

I knew that Mr. Bingley was right, and yet I could not help but hope that perhaps I could keep it a secret just a little while longer. There was no version of events, no place on earth, no means by which my mother would consent to my solving mysteries with anyone, and especially not someone she detested as much as Mr. Holmes.

"I shall think on it," I told him. "I can't promise you anything more than that at this moment, Charles."

It still felt odd to call my brother-in-law by his first name, despite my being the one to suggest it. But I did want to be more intimate with him. Mr. Bingley had made a fine husband for Jane and they were as enamored of one another now as they had been when they had first met. If anything could induce me to consider marriage, it would be the example that Mr. Bingley and my dear Jane set. If such a connection should happen to me, then perhaps I should not be opposed to the notion. But until then, I was quite happy to pursue my career alongside Mr. Holmes.

In any case, I desired Mr. Bingley's friendship and I hoped that he felt the same about me. I made a small promise to myself to call him Charles more often to show him my deep regard.

Having heard my reply, Mr. Bingley looked as though he wished to sigh, or perhaps speak again, but then was thinking better of it. "It is, of course, your choice. Jane and I cannot will anything upon you. We're not your parents and we respect your independence. I almost wish my own sisters…"

Here a look of pain crossed Mr. Bingley's face. It was there and gone in a moment, but I saw it and knew it for what it was. The nasty business, to use my mother's words, of Mr. Wickham's murder had been carried out by Mr. Bingley's sister. Mrs. Hurst, his married sister, all but refused to see Mr. Bingley since the events and Mr. Bingley's marriage to Jane. Miss Bingley, the one who had committed the crime, was currently in prison. We all knew what fate would eventually befall her.

I had never spoken to Mr. Bingley on the matter. I am quite sure that Jane had, seeing as they were husband and wife and none are so good at soothing and comforting as my dear Jane. Sometimes I wanted to offer comfort of my own, but I was never any good at it, at least in my own opinion. There was also the not-insignificant matter of my having helped Mr. Holmes in discovering it was Miss Bingley who had organized the murder.

Before I could rightly arrange my thoughts or offer something up, anything to say by way of alieving Mr. Bingley's distress, the moment had passed and Mr. Bingley looked himself again.

"In any case," he finished, as though he had not stopped, "I felt that although the decision is yours, it would be prudent for me to state my thoughts."

"And I appreciate you doing so," I told him, for truly I did. Mr. Bingley gave me advice in such a respectful way, not like my mother, who did so expecting to be obeyed. "I will think on it, as I said. I need a day to think on what's best."

"Understandable." Mr. Bingley then caught up his hat. "I am stepping out, but you'll find Jane much as you left her." He said it with a knowing tone and I suspected that he knew more of Jane's frustrations with her state than he thought she did.

I said goodbye to my brother-in-law and hurried to find Jane. I did not tell her what had transpired at Mr. Holmes' flat to make me come home so much sooner than usual, and was happy to occupy myself with reading to her and helping her with correspondence. Yet despite the joy of spending time with my dearest companion, I couldn't help but feel guilt gnawing at me.

It confused me, I admit. I did not know why I should be feeling guilty. I had done nothing wrong. Or had I? As I have previously confessed, I have a rather selfish nature at times. More than once I have been blinded by prejudice. But what had I done that would merit feelings of guilt?

Perhaps it was that I was keeping such a secret from the rest of my family. Perhaps I should tell Mother, despite the fallout that would inevitably come from it. She would never approve and never understand. I didn't need her to understand. I didn't need anyone to understand. But it would be pleasant to have her support in my chosen course in life.

These thoughts followed me to bed and continued to chase me when I rose the next day. At first, I considered not calling upon Mr. Holmes. We had parted on rather harsh terms yesterday after all. But then I remembered the scarred man from the day before and how he had accosted me. He had known who I was as well as who Mr. Holmes was. At the very least, I must ask Mr. Holmes about the matter, either to be enlightened or to warn him. For the time being I shoved aside all feelings of guilt and made my way to 221B Baker Street.

Mrs. Hudson was glad to see me when I knocked on the door. "Miss Bennet, a pleasure as always! Are you quite all right, dear? You left in a bit of a hurry yesterday."

It appeared that my rattled nature had not gone unnoticed. "I had to return home," I admitted without telling her why, "but I'm quite well, I assure you. I appreciate the concern, Mrs. Hudson. Is Mr. Holmes about?"

"I'm afraid I don't quite know," Mrs. Hudson admitted, "But then I never do quite know with that man. Sometimes I go up to do a spot of cleaning thinking he's gone out and there he is lurking about and scaring me half to death. Then other times I'm certain he's home and I go up to speak with him and he's not there."

"That does sound like Mr. Holmes." I saw no reason for him not to be there, however, seeing as these were his regular office hours and he was accustomed to my arrival.

Unless our rather pointed discussion the day before had changed that. The guilt returned to my stomach and I thought that perhaps I had been too harsh in my words to Mr. Holmes. I knew that he did not care for what impression he made upon others and I shouldn't have assumed that a simple lecture would explain to him that while he might not care what others thought, we had to make a good impression upon clients so that we continued to get them. And perhaps I had behaved a bit like a mother to him, assuming a position of authority that I did not have.

I resolved to bury the hatchet and apologize and perhaps find a more tactful way of explaining the need for the flat to be properly cleaned, only to open the door and find that Mr. Holmes was not there.

But the scarred man was.

He was dressed in the same garb as yesterday and was standing in front of the fire, idly picking at his coat. He turned as I entered and gave me a distrusting look. I could observe in his stance from the way he planted his feet wide and sank his weight, as if anticipating a fight, and how his chest curved inward away from me, that he did not like my presence.

Well, the feeling was quite mutual.

I hovered in the doorway. "What are you doing here?" I asked. Or rather, demanded. "Where is Mr. Holmes?"

"I think I could ask you the same question, Elizabeth."

"Miss Bennet, if you please," I replied. "You clearly know who I am. At least give me the courtesy of addressing me properly. Sir." I added the last word as a pointed rebuke.

The man merely gave me a wolfish smile. It reminded me of a starving animal that has at last found a good meal. To say it disconcerted me would be an understatement. I had never before considered that any of Mr. Holmes' potential clients would be anything other than those of the middle and upper classes, especially considering the fees that he charged. The idea of someone of this nature calling had not once entered my mind.

Now I saw the folly of that thinking. Mr. Holmes solved crimes and he was not a member of Scotland Yard. Who better to consult, in the minds of the criminal classes? If they had a grievance but were criminals themselves and could not go to the police, a so-called consulting detective could be their best bet.

Although I must admit that the man's state of dress did not suggest someone who could afford Mr. Holmes' fees.

The two of us stood at opposite ends of the room like that for goodness knows how long. I was poised to flee the moment the man took a step towards me, and wished myself closer to the fireplace so that I could grab a poker as a weapon if need be. The scarred man, however, seemed just as wary of me and watched me with both a sort of hunger and distrust. The first I put down to his eagerness about Mr. Holmes and my being his associate. The latter I saw no reason for. He was the one imposing himself in another man's home and accosting women.

I wondered if perhaps I should have further considered the implications of working with Mr. Holmes beforehand. I loved observing and seeing what I could learn about people and the world by simply using my mind, but I had no wish to be in danger or to hurt my family by being assaulted myself.

As these thoughts came to me, there was the telltale sound of footsteps outside. The scared man and I both turned our heads towards the noise, although I still kept him in the corner of my vision and he appeared to do the same.

Holmes entered and immediately paused. "I thought that I might find you two in such a state."

"Mr. Holmes," I said, "would you care to tell me who this man is?"

"Oh, yes, do tell," the man added. "I would be delighted to see if your powers are as supernatural as I've heard."

Mr. Holmes looked over at me. I could not read his expression. He was one of the few people that I still could not always observe with accuracy, and so I was not sure what he was trying to communicate to me, if he was trying to communicate anything at all.

Then he turned back to our guest. "You are a businessman and a leader and used to being obeyed."

The man gave a small bow. "All quite true."

"It shows in your bearing and your manner," Mr. Holmes said dismissively. "I would also venture to say that your business is frowned upon by the good people of London and the law. Something in the business of entertainment, I should think, but not prostitution."

I bit my lip hard to keep from letting out a sound at his blunt words. Mr. Holmes still surprised me with how forthright he was in his language. Not that he was a crude man, merely one that thought it best to get into the heart of the matter and that honest, blunt language was the best means to do so.

I expected more but Mr. Holmes waved his hand. “But my time has already been wasted today. I won’t play anymore. I wish for you to tell me why you’re here. Because of a crime, of course, but there is something odd about it. Especially considering how you accosted my associate, Miss Bennet, yesterday.”

I could not hold in my surprise. “I was not aware that you knew of that.”

“I am always aware of what my close associates are up to,” Mr. Holmes replied. I chose to take this as a sign that he cared for my wellbeing. Perhaps this was Mr. Holmes’ equivalent of how Jane always knew the right things to say when I was upset or how Father always had a choice passage from a book to read to me.

“Now, if you please,” Mr. Holmes continued, gesturing to the man. “If you would tell us your business.”

I saw the gleam in his eye and knew that for all of his bluster, Mr. Holmes was interested in this case. It must have been the one that he had spoken of to me yesterday. If this was the client, then I could better understand Mr. Holmes not caring about the state of his flat.

The man gave a small, theatrical bow once again. “I go by many names,” he began, “but the one I use the most as of late is Dr. Barnabus. I run a little show of sorts. All good and fun entertainment.

Perhaps you have heard of it? The Good Doctor's Show?"

I looked at Mr. Holmes, for I must confess that I had never heard of such a show. But then, I suspected that no one of my circle would have ever heard of anything put on by this Dr. Barnabus. Mr. Holmes' face gave away nothing.

After a moment, Dr. Barnabus went on. "Recently I have had reason to require your services. Money is of no object, but time is of the essence."

"I suppose you will not tell us what the crime is," I said, rather out of character. Usually it was Mr. Holmes who lost patience with our clients while I took on the task of soothing them. This odious man, however, was most trying to my patience.

"He cannot tell us what the crime is," Mr. Holmes pronounced, "because it has not occurred yet."

Dr. Barnabus laughed. It was a harsh, grating sound, as though his voice had been coated in rust. "Precisely. I see that your reputation is not inflated!"

He produced from his pocket two tickets, which he then held out to Mr. Holmes. "I beseech you to come and see one of my shows for yourself. Only after you have witnessed it will I be able to fully explain to you my fears."

Mr. Holmes studied the tickets for a moment. Without looking up, he said, "We shall take this into due consideration. If you would give my associate and myself some time, we have other business to discuss. You will know our answer to your case if you see us at the show."

Dr. Barnabus gave another of those disconcerting smiles and made his way to the door. "Of course. Oh, and Miss Elizabeth?"

"Miss Bennet," I corrected him.

"Ah, yes. I do hope your sister is faring well. First pregnancies are often the hardest. She must take care to look after her health."

With that pronouncement, he swept out the door, leaving me in a fit of anger and fear.

# CHAPTER FOUR:

## An Agreement

Once Dr. Barnabus left, my knees almost buckled beneath me. First, he knew my name and my association with Mr. Holmes, all of which was concerning enough, but now he knew of Jane and her condition. Was his comment about her health a threat? Was he putting my sister in danger? Was I putting my sister in danger by continuing to work with Mr. Holmes?

"You are distressed," Mr. Holmes stated. As usual, it was not a question with him.

"Did you not just hear what that man said?" I asked. My heart felt as though it would beat right out of my ribcage. "He knows of my sister. Her pregnancy. I can let harm come to me but it shall never come to her. Never."

Even as I spoke those words, I knew them to be true. I would not seek out danger or risk, but if it came, I would meet it with a head held high. But nothing, nothing in the world could come to harm my Jane. The thought of someone denying her happiness was bad enough, as I had once experienced when I learned that Miss Bingley's murder of Mr. Wickham had happened at the time that it did in order to prevent Mr. Bingley from marrying my Jane. It was not Miss Bingley's original reason for murdering the philandering rake, but it was an added reason and sped her murderous intent along. And all to keep Jane away from her brother because of our family, when anyone with eyes could see how they loved one another almost from the first moment. I couldn't stand the idea of someone getting in between Jane and happiness. The idea of someone actually physically harming her or her unborn child sickened me to the quick and filled me with an anger I had never known.

"This *supposed* doctor was not threatening your sister," Mr. Holmes said. "He was trying to demonstrate his power. This is a man used to being in charge and being obeyed." He paused. "No, not obeyed. Worshipped. He is used to people being in awe of him. He wished for you to feel the same way. In speaking of your sister, he only wanted to show you how clever and powerful he was. He could gain nothing by harming Jane or threatening you."

His words calmed me. Mr. Holmes was not the sort of man to lie or soften the truth to spare a person's feelings. Quite the opposite. If he did not think that Jane was in danger, then I could relax.

"I take it by your use of the word 'supposed' that you do not think he possesses any kind of degree, either."

"Correct. It is a showman's title." Mr. Holmes rustled through the inner pockets of his coat. "I apologize for my lateness. I had difficulty in finding what I sought."

The apology was unusual, but before I could comment on it, Mr. Holmes found what he sought and held it out to me. It was a poster, grimy with dirt and a bit faded, but still eye-catching. It read:

*The Good Doctor's Show! Come and see the wonders of this world and the world beyond, brought by the esteemed and mysterious Dr. Barnabus and his crew of mystics and wonders. You will have to see to believe!*

"It's all a crock," I said, using a word I had picked up from Mrs. Hudson. "A silly side circus."

"Silly to you, perhaps, but to Dr. Barnabus, it is his life," Mr. Holmes replied. "The sort of audience he draws in with these posters in unsavory parts of town are undoubtedly unsavory themselves, as well as poor folk in dire need of a distraction. To their small minds, he can play God, and he revels in it."

"You speak as though you know him intimately."

"I know his kind," Mr. Holmes corrected.

That was how people were to Mr. Holmes. There was no individual, but rather one example of a certain sort or type. I sometimes wondered if I myself fell into a category like everyone else. This didn't seem to mean that Mr. Holmes valued a person any less. He was kind in his way to Mr. Bingley and had always strived to be fastidious in his manners to Jane, although he had once gone to lengths to explain to me how and why they were quite boring and ordinary. Yet I couldn't help but hope that he saw me as different, as singular. Not that I wished to be treated as a pet or prodigy or as a wife, but my pride pricked at me to think that I was still just one of many, especially to someone who had opened my eyes to such a new world and to my own abilities.

Yet I knew that I would never have the courage to ask him about such a thing. I was simply not courageous in that way. In fact, I often wondered if

I was courageous at all. Would not the courageous thing to do be to tell my mother of the truth and hang the consequences?

"Your mind is drifting," Mr. Holmes remarked.

"I apologize," I said, but I offered no further explanation. "Are we to attend this show, then?"

"Yes, I should think so," Mr. Holmes said. "This case is finally an interesting one. A crime that has not yet been committed but is only suspected, I have not stumbled across one of those yet."

"You speak as though they happen regularly," I observed as I crossed over to the kitchen area to see what I could do about cleaning up the place while Mr. Holmes was distracted.

"I'm sure that they do, but people rarely bother to ask someone for help with them," Mr. Holmes explained. "We all have what the layman calls intuition or a sixth sense, but what you and I know is observation. To the untrained brain, these observations of small tells in a person's behavior or of the world around us are not consciously noticed. They are subconsciously noticed instead, which leads to a vague feeling of suspicion and concern. We can't exactly pinpoint what made us concerned or suspicious, we only know that the feeling is there. We suddenly know that something bad is going to happen, and sometimes we even know what that bad thing is: someone is going to steal from us, or someone is going to murder us. But what would be the point in going to the police about it? We have nothing but our convictions."

"Or in this case," I said, "we bring our convictions to a consulting detective."

Mr. Holmes nodded and I turned to focus back on the kitchen. To my surprise, it was tidied up. Not spotless and certainly not to the level of cleanliness I had seen in the kitchen back at Longbourn when I would sneak down to wheedle treats out of our cook, but neater than I had seen Mr. Holmes' kitchen since I had started working with him.

Knowing that he would have observed my realization, I skipped over stating the obvious, something Mr. Holmes hated, and merely said, "Mr. Holmes, why did you bother cleaning when you made it apparent how little you care for it?"

Mr. Holmes cleared his throat. "It occurred to me that your argument had merit. I do not care what our clients think of *me*, but clients will not come if they find the *place* distasteful."

"I was scolding in my manner," I said, the apology I had half-thought of delivering tripping out of my mouth before I could think and worry over it any further. "I should not have spoken to you in that way." I tried to think of an agreement that would please us both. "I cannot clean up after you constantly. I am not your housemaid. But I can't force you to do anything that you dislike, either."

"A fair observation." Mr. Holmes situated himself in his favorite chair by the fire. "Perhaps I can attempt to keep my mess to a minimum and you can agree to clean up that mess, provided it is indeed a small one?"

I did not object to a bit of tidying up if the amount was manageable and not the appalling mold-infested sort that I had stumbled across before. "That sounds like a fair agreement, Mr. Holmes."

"My moods," Mr. Holmes began. He then paused. He seemed to be struggling for words. This was unlike him. "I know that I am not the easiest person to get along with, Miss Bennet. You must not take personal offense when I act as I did yesterday. If you are willing to weather those small storms, I can continue to have you as my associate. I would like to have you," he added, correcting himself.

"That sounds just fine to me," I told him.

"Good, good," Mr. Holmes nodded. "Now, about your mother…"

I sighed. "Mr. Holmes, I am not even going to begin to ask how you know about this matter."

Mr. Holmes gave me one of his very small smiles, just a tiny upturn of the lips. They were quite rare and I always felt pleased when he gave them to me, for they usually signified that I had made an astute observation. "Homeless network. They overhear the most fascinating things."

There was nothing to do, I thought, except to make us some tea and bite hard on my tongue to prevent another argument.

"Also, Miss Bennet," Mr. Holmes added, "I think we must find some clothes for you to borrow for tonight."

"Clothes?" I asked. "Whatever for?"

The dress I was wearing was quite plain and I would never be seen in it outside of the house back home where everyone knew everyone and all ladies constantly judged one another on their state of dress. Here in London, I could get away with a certain level of anonymity and therefore a certain level of simplicity in my fabrics. Despite that, however, the cut was flattering and the quality of fabric good and I thought it quite suitable for whatever social setting we were likely to find ourselves in.

"You look too much like a lady, Miss Bennet," Mr. Holmes said. He sounded amused. "Where we are going, we cannot afford to be recognized, whether as a consulting detective or as the sort of woman who is the sister-in-law of a man with five thousand a year."

I supposed that Mr. Holmes did have a point. The sort of people he talked of attending Dr. Barnabus's show would not take kindly to one of my social class in their midst. Or at the very least, I would stand out like a sheep in a wolves' den. Pick-pockets and other similar sorts were sure to be about and I didn't want to invite them to come and sample my purse.

"Very well," I said. "I don't suppose you have suitable clothes on hand?" I turned to look and saw that Mr. Holmes already had some items in hand, which he was laying out on a spare table.

"I shall wear a disguise as well," Mr. Holmes added. "It has been some time since I've employed such methods. I think it will be enjoyable."

I could hardly stifle a laugh. Only Mr. Holmes would say that putting on a disguise and watching a seedy magician's show was enjoyable. It was clear that as his associate I would never have a dull moment.

# CHAPTER FIVE:

## *The Show*

Mr. Holmes and I had weathered our first true argument since the beginning of our partnership and had come to a satisfactory agreement regarding the issue. That, I felt, was a good step forward in our relationship. But I knew then that it would not be the last argument that we ever had. We were both proud and stubborn people, neither of us inclined to admit when we were wrong. It was only a matter of time before one of us crossed the other, or we crossed each other, and it would take our wounded pride some time to allow us to apologize to each other.

There were times, however, when no amount of pride can overcome the practicality of one's situation. It was prudent that we go in disguise, and so we did. But had anyone who knew me seen me then, I should have hidden away in embarrassment.

Mr. Holmes had used a careful application of putty and powder upon himself to change his face to make him appear much changed. His nose was longer and fatter, his chin thicker, and his eyebrows drawn together. He had worked over my face in a similar way to give me bushy eyebrows and a good few pockmarks, my nose made to imitate the shape of his and the tone of my skin changed.

"We look like brother and sister, do we not?" Mr. Holmes noted, holding the mirror up for my inspection.

I thought that I looked rather a horror. I looked like someone who took no care in their appearance and I found myself a bit appalled that I should care that much for someone's features. But I did have a rather nice face, and I'd been told that I had rather fine eyes, and it gave me more distress than I would have thought to see it modified into something so plain and distasteful. But I could not deny that I did not look like myself, and that was the purpose of going through all of this.

"We do look related," I admitted, for Mr. Holmes had done our faces up similarly.

Satisfied with this, Mr. Holmes set down the mirror and helped me into my coat, one of the few gentlemanly gestures he regularly employed.

We set out for the location stated on the poster Mr. Holmes had found. I personally wondered how Dr. Barnabus thought we were to discover his show if he didn't tell us where it was, but perhaps he thought he could rely upon Mr. Holmes' observational skills for that. Mr. Holmes in fact told me as we walked of the few things he had noticed about Dr. Barnabus that told him the general area the show was held in, an area where the train ran through and there was a tin factory.

The area was unlike any that I had been to before, even with Mr. Holmes. Previously we had gone to the homes of our clients and to the scenes of crimes, but the worst so far had been a few alleyways for the latter and plain but clean homes for the former. Nothing could have prepared me for the horrid sights and smells as we made our way through the increasingly poor streets. If Mother could have seen me like this, she would have fainted dead away. A real faint, and not one of her exaggerated ones.

I could tell when we were getting close to the show, for a strange haunting music was playing, beckoning people to come and take a peek. It was probably supposed to be inviting, to spark curiosity, but it struck me as chilling.

"There is another reason," Mr. Holmes admitted, "for our disguise tonight, Miss Bennet." He helped guide me around a puddle containing who knew what distasteful things. "I do not fully trust our employer."

"Oh?" I asked, trying to focus on Mr. Holmes' words and not on the chill creeping up my spine.

"Every entertainment has a history," Mr. Holmes explained. "You can trail its way through the cities and backwaters of the country. Yet none of my homeless network can give me a solid trail of this supposed show. It is as if it appeared out of thin air."

"You think that perhaps it is a trap?" I asked. A trap for whom and for what purpose, I did not know, but I did not like the thought. I was again reminded that this life was more dangerous than I had previously thought.

"We shall see," Mr. Holmes said, his voice a bit grimmer than usual.

We followed the sound of the music to an open stockyard sort of area. There were train tracks making a kind of border at one end and buildings on the other three sides. In the middle, a dark red tent of sorts had been erected. To my concern, we saw no one else entering the tent.

Mr. Holmes paused, and as I had taken his arm when we had set out on our journey, I too paused in my tracks.

"Are you quite sure of this?" I asked, fear lancing through me properly for the first time. I had never before been afraid. Oh, there had been moments. These past few weeks, it felt like I was in a constant state over Jane. But it was nothing like this. It was as if I was one of those people that Mr. Holmes had spoken of, those people who observe something small that tells them there is danger but do not realize they observe it and so are left with nothing but this sixth sense of dread.

"Yes," Mr. Holmes said. He nodded briskly, suddenly all business. "Let us proceed, Miss Bennet."

We walked into the tent.

Inside, we saw several wooden seats had been set up. There were others seated about, and I was relieved to find that Mr. Holmes and I would not be the only ones after all. The people seated looked rather as Mr. Holmes and I did, that is, they were of the lower classes. Many of them appeared to have not bathed in some time. I was glad when Mr. Holmes chose us a seat that was away from any others. The presence of other people was comforting but I did not need to be any closer to someone who might eavesdrop on us at the wrong moment and would smell unpleasant as well.

In front of the seats, which were arranged in a sort of V shape, was an empty and sandy area that had quite obviously been raked over and cleaned for such an occasion. The rest of the ground outside was a hodgepodge of different sands and rocks and gravel, and stained with various puddles and goodness knows what sort of vile substances. Scraps of trash were littered about everywhere there. In the stage area, for I assumed that was what it must be, the larger bits of gravel had been cleared away and all manner of trash and stains removed to create a somewhat smooth and uniform performing area.

As we took our seats and settled ourselves, the area around the audience began to dim while the area of cleared sand became brighter. It was clear that the show was about to begin. I tried not to shift too much while seated next to Mr. Holmes. This entire affair was making me concerned. I could not shake the feeling of foreboding.

Mr. Holmes did not seem to be affected with the same sort of concern that held me, or if he was, he did not show it. He seemed to be analyzing, his eyes narrowing slightly and his lips thinning as he pressed them together. While I saw something I could not quite describe that made my heart race, Mr. Holmes saw a puzzle that needed to be solved. I hoped to someday reach the point where I could see the world in the same way that he did.

The music changed from the tune I had heard before to something a little more upbeat, something with fanfare. There was a clap as if thunder was sounding in the room, and a flash, and then a puff of billowing smoke in the center of the stage. Out of it stepped our mysterious client, the supposed Dr. Barnabus. He had now changed his appearance to something of a showman, wearing a coat and waistcoat that both matched the dark red color of the tent. He spread his arms wide and bowed to us all, a smile on his face that reminded me of the way foxes looked at hens in my childhood books about talking animals.

Dr. Barnabus waved at all of us invitingly and then began to speak. "It is my great honor to address all of you here today."

His voice was different than before, done in an affected manner. The way he shaped the vowels was changed, rounding out some and clipping others, whereas before they had been swallowed and mushed about in his mouth.

Mr. Holmes leaned in as Dr. Barnabus continued his opening speech. "What do you observe, Miss Bennet?"

He had asked me that question many times before, and as always, I strove to answer him as intelligently as I could. "He's putting on a voice, and a very good one. If I had not met him before, I should not have realized that it was not his natural voice."

"Yes, and it is always harder to affect a polished voice than to affect a thick one," Mr. Holmes observed. "What else?"

My gazed darted over Dr. Barnabus, trying to take in all of him and see what I could learn from it. "His clothes are of a fine fabric, finer than I would have thought, but old. Well cared-for, but certainly worn, I should think he got them second-hand or has been using them for some time."

"It is one or the other, Miss Bennet," Mr. Holmes said. "Second-hand or used by Dr. Barnabus himself. Which do you think?"

I took in the shape of the clothes and how they lay against the man's frame. "I should say second-hand. To buy such good cloth first-hand, he would have bothered to get them tailored to his measurements. Otherwise, why bother with the fabric at all? Such an outfit is an investment. His clothes are well-suited and I do not think that anyone else here would notice it, but I confess I am used to the exact measurements that are used on the men I have grown up with. They fit but they are not tailored, so I would venture to say second-hand."

"Well done, Miss Bennet," Mr. Holmes acknowledged. I felt a rush of pride and the thrill of excitement as I always did when I successfully solved a bit of the puzzle that made up a human being. "Well-made, fine clothes that he got second hand and yet somehow distinctly match the tent fabric. Interesting indeed. And what can you say about our audience?"

Dr. Barnabus was finishing up his speech. "And now, allow me to perform the first trick for you—but this is no trick, ladies and gentlemen, or at least not the kind of trick that you would be used to. This is serious and you must pay close attention."

I looked around at the scattered audience members. "They are none of them very attentive," I noted. One or two of them appeared genuinely curious but most seemed to simply be sitting there for the sake of a place to rest. Yet these were people who had not a penny to spare if we were to go by appearances. Why would they waste their entrance fee if they did not care about the show?

"It is rather odd," I began, "but if I did not know any better, I would say that the audience doesn't care a whit about the show."

"I agree," Mr. Holmes said. "And it is most concerning."

"It is?" I turned to look at him. "Concerning how?"

"And now!" Dr. Barnabus announced. "The sleep of death!"

The words were ominous and my head snapped up to look at Dr. Barnabus, my instincts screaming at me that this was quite wrong, but I only had time to feel alarm flash through me at his words before I smelled something that was sweet to the point of being sickly. The room spun around me and I thought I heard a crash in the distance, and perhaps some yelling, but then I was descending into blackness and I knew nothing else.

# CHAPTER SIX:

## The Entrapment

I came to in pieces, rather like a jigsaw puzzle. First, I became aware that I was awake. That was all, no senses quite on board yet. I simply knew that I had been asleep and that I was no longer in such a state. Next, I became aware of my body and how heavy it felt and in such an odd way. It was nothing like when I woke up from a deep sleep and felt that pleasant heaviness in my limbs. This was a dull weight, like my limbs were not quite mine yet.

And the headache! My poor head did ache something fierce. I could only blink at first as lights began to dance in front of my vision. It all only made my head feel so much worse.

Everything was a dull throb for a moment, and then it all began to clear bit by bit. I could move my limbs. The blurred colored lights in front of me slowly joined together and became crisp and firmly outlined, turning into proper shapes that then turned into people and objects.

It was then that I became aware that I was restrained.

"It really is a pity that your Mr. Holmes is so clever," spoke a familiar voice.

I managed to turn my head a bit and in the process realized that I was bound to a chair. It was rickety and I hoped that it managed to hold my weight and my shifting about. If it was to fall to pieces I didn't think that it would lead to my freedom but rather to my rather undignified sprawl onto the floor.

"Ah, yes, you'll want to see me." The person speaking took a step so that he could be in my line of sight, and I recognized both him and his voice.

It was Dr. Barnabus.

I waited for a moment for an explanation. I was not gagged and I was not bound at my feet so that I could shift as I wished for comfort's sake, but my hands were around the back of the chair and secured quite tightly. I had no experience with knots of this sort but I had a feeling that even if I had been, that experience would be useless against the complicated ties my hands now found themselves in.

When Dr. Barnabus did not provide an answer, I looked around. Mr. Holmes was nowhere to be seen and I vaguely recalled what sounded like a scuffle as I had spun into unconsciousness. I was now on the stage part of the sand and gravel. The benches had been cleared out and stood empty, save for one or two grim-faced men sitting on one of the benches in the front row. Neither of them looked like the sort to have sympathy for me. They were dressed rather shabbily, one of them heavyset with hooded eyes and the other paper-thin and pale with a triangular face and pointed chin. They made quite the contrast in size and appearance and at another time I might have found it amusing. Now it just was another useless observation.

Observing, the thought came to me, that was what I should be doing. I must figure out what was going on. I focused more on the two men on the benches. The heavyset one was outright glaring at me with a clenched jaw and I could clearly see a small knife in his hand. He was trying to scare me, I realized. His clothes were just a bit too small, his shirt stretched wide over his barrel chest. Too poor to afford clothes that properly fit, and perhaps with a slight issue of gluttony. Despite the firm muscles I could see in his arms and legs, he had a bit of a potbelly. Sweets, most likely. I doubted he had the funds for truly rich food for meals but a bit of spare coin for candy was easy to come by.

The second man, so thin and pale, seemed nervous, although he was doing his best to hide it. He kept glancing over at Dr. Barnabus as if for guidance. His right fist was dug into the pants leg at his upper right thigh and I could see his fingers flexing around it every so often in a nervous tick. His clothes were neatly pressed and cleaned but looked threadbare. Fastidious about his appearance, but without money to afford proper clothes.

Neither of these men looked like the sort of coarse thug that would harm a lady at a moment's notice, but I still ought to tread carefully. I also still had no idea what to make of Dr. Barnabus, who was determined, it seemed at least to me, to put on a show of intimidation.

"As I said, it really is a pity all around that your associate is so good at what he does," Dr. Barnabus said.

He wore the same clothes as he had during the show. Up close, I could see where the seams and buttons and so on had needed repairing over the years. Overall, I thought, the look suited him better than his awful attire from our first two meetings.

He continued, "Our original plan was quite gentlemanly, I assure you."

"I'm afraid that you will have to enlighten me," I said. "For I admit that I have no idea what you are talking about."

I supposed that honesty was the best policy in this instance. I could tell that the two gentlemen watching me were Dr. Barnabus's hired men, not used to having someone at their disposal to possibly harm, but that was all I could make out. I was sure that Mr. Holmes could have done far better than I was doing.

Dr. Barnabus sighed, as though explaining this was quite trying on his time. I saw through this, for his eyes lit up rather in the same way that Mr. Holmes' did when he had an interesting case. "I was hired by a rather powerful man to investigate your Mr. Holmes and see if he was as good as he claimed to be. If he was, or perhaps even if he wasn't, we were to break into his flat and gather what information about him we could and then report it. Unfortunately, Mr. Holmes has an uncanny knack for knowing when we were going to stop by, or he keeps a very erratic schedule."

Personally, I suspected that it was a little of both. Mr. Holmes must have known that someone was after him, but I doubted that his schedule was any more regular on days when he didn't have somebody on his tail. His office hours were the only consistency and I had a feeling that even that was a recent development in order to accommodate me.

"It was then decided among us that we would devise a means of distracting Mr. Holmes in order to keep him out of his flat long enough for us to gather the necessary information," Dr. Barnabus went on. "If we could get information out of the man himself in the meantime, so much the better."

It was so subtle that I almost missed it, but I saw the way that the heavyset man clenched his jaw when Dr. Barnabus said that 'it was decided.' I remembered how Mr. Holmes had spoken of Dr. Barnabus being a man who wanted power over others. Perhaps this course of action had not been universally decided upon, but rather dictated.

"There was never a case," I said, my mind whirring as I tried to devise a means to secure my release. "You made one up to distract Mr. Holmes. You made up the entire show as well, that was why Mr. Holmes could find no record of it."

"You are a clever one," Dr. Barnabus acknowledged. "It really is a pity that we'll have to do away with you after all of this."

My blood ran cold. Perhaps some heroes and heroines could face death with a certain measure of honor and grace, but I fully intended to go to my grave spitting and yowling like an awful tomcat. I had no wish to die. I would never see Jane again, and I would never have the chance to see her darling baby, my first niece or nephew. I would never see Kitty and Lydia and Mary again, the sisters that I was only just starting to appreciate. I would die before my father, which was not how the world should work. I would never want to cause Father distress and here I would be bringing him the ultimate grief. I even felt distress for Mother. After what had happened to Lydia, I felt quite certain that anything happening to me would be more than her poor nerves could stand.

I tried to make sure that none of this fear showed on my face. I loved life and I loved the joy of it. There was nothing I liked better than a laugh. But these men couldn't know that. I didn't want them to see they had such a hold on me.

"The other audience members were bored. I assume you paid them to come and see the show so that Mr. Holmes and I were not the only ones?"

"We did have one or two people wander in out of curiosity," Dr. Barnabus acknowledged. "But they were sent away along with everyone else. We gave them a lighter dose of the chloroform than we gave you so they would wake up sooner and we deposited them a bit away. They should all have woken up in various areas about town confused, but none the wiser."

"Did you originally intend for me to wake up like this?" I asked. "Or did the struggle that Mr. Holmes started change the plan?"

Dr. Barnaby sighed like a long-suffering martyr. "The plan was to put you out and to give you just a dash of opium with the dose so that you had fantastical dreams. You would think that it was the show and then afterwards I should have a case that I had made up for you that you could solve. Mr. Holmes should never have been the wiser about what we were up to. But he figured it out anyway. I could see it in his eyes. I gave a small signal to my men here," and Dr. Barnaby indicated the two men on the bench, "and they simply tried to give you chloroform. Mr. Holmes, as you seem to know, fought back."

"And escaped," I added. I could not entertain the other thought—that he was dead. "You don't have him."

"Yes, but my boys at his flat will deal with him." Dr. Barnabus sounded dismissive. "The trouble is now dealing with you. It pains me to say that we must do away with you, Elizabeth, really it does."

"Miss Bennet," I corrected with a sigh of frustration. "If you are to do away with me, as you have stated twice now, I would appreciate it if you would respect my wishes and address me in the proper manner."

"Does a lady running about with the likes of Mr. Holmes truly deserve to be addressed properly?" Dr. Barnabus asked. "Think of the rather low, criminal class you are speaking with right at this very moment. I doubt your family would be proud if they saw you in your current situation."

They would be far from proud, which I was sure that Dr. Barnabus could figure out for himself. But that had nothing to do with class. I doubted that any parent wanted their daughter or any sibling wanted their sister to be tied and with their life being threatened.

"Who is your employer?" I asked. "And why go through all of this trouble? Why all of this subterfuge, this elaborate scheme? Surely if he was interested in Mr. Holmes, he could inquire about him on his own time. I know that Mr. Holmes is of a certain difficult turn of mind at times, but your employer could have solved all of this by coming to see Mr. Holmes for himself."

"That would mean revealing himself to Mr. Holmes, however inadvertently," Dr. Barnabus explained this all to me patiently, if not a bit patronizingly. "Mr. Holmes is not the type of man to forget a face or a voice and our employer did not want to give him occasion to remember either should their paths cross at a later date."

"He seems to want something from Mr. Holmes," I hazarded. "He has gone through a great deal of trouble to learn about him through you. Surely he would not want Mr. Holmes dead, in that case."

"I never said that Mr. Holmes would end up sharing the same fate as you," Dr. Barnabus pointed out. "When I said that my men at his flat would take care of him, I simply meant that they would incapacitate him. It is unfortunate that he now knows he has an enemy, rather than not knowing he had one at all, but alas. You, however, are considered expendable to our employer. Mr. Holmes can easily find a new pet with which he can entertain himself." He smiled at me. "I do hope that you said a proper goodbye to your sister this morning, Elizabeth."

# CHAPTER SEVEN:

## Elizabeth Negotiates

My heart raced. I glanced over at the two men on the bench. The heavyset one still clenched his jaw and there was a tightness to his muscles. He didn't like this course of action, I thought. He didn't want to hurt me. That gave me hope.

I looked over at the other one, the thin man. He was still fidgety, seeking guidance. He could go either way, I thought. He would side with whichever one showed the strongest spirit.

Perhaps I was not lost after all.

"Murdering the daughter of a gentleman is not the wisest of ideas," I pointed out to Dr. Barnabus. "My brother-in-law, as I'm sure you know, is a man of considerable money and wealth, and he has friends that are just as powerful, if not more so, than he is. I would think twice before entering into the kind of mess that my death would lead to for you."

"You say that as if young women do not vanish all the time in London," Dr. Barnabus said. "I know that in a small place such as where you grew up such things must be a great cause for hullabaloo, if they happen at all, but here it is commonplace. More commonplace than most people of your class like to admit, I'm afraid. Your family, I'm sure, will do what they can, but what evidence is there? What can be done?"

"You will make a fevered enemy of Mr. Holmes," I said. I kept my voice measured and did my best to hide the fear I felt growing in my heart. "He is demon enough when he is arguing about the dishes. I don't think I should care to risk his wrath about a matter as important as this. He has many more powerful friends than my brother-in-law. Judges and others in charge of the courts are in his debt. He is owed large favors by prominent, rich people and he is a determined man. Even if I admit that my family's efforts would go unrewarded, his would not."

"I think that we should listen to her," the heavyset man admitted. "She's making sense. It would be too big of a risk."

"We can't let her go, knowing all that she knows," Dr. Barnabus replied dismissively.

"She didn't know nearly as much until you started talking to her about it," the man said. He stood up. "You didn't have to tell her about anything and there you were, going on about it like you were Hamlet in the final bit where he says why he did it all to his uncle."

I would not have thought this man acquainted with the works of Shakespeare. I was pleasantly surprised. But more than that, I was pleased. My plan was working and the two men were starting to turn against each other. The third man looked between them, and seemed upset. He would have to choose one of them soon if the conversation continued in this vein. I could only hope that he chose the side of my unknown ally.

"We must tie up all loose ends," Dr. Barnabus replied. "And I am the leader here."

"You're the leader by default. Any one of us could replace you at any time, I reckon. Same way pirate captains got replaced if the crew didn't like them," the heavyset man said.

"Now, Johnson, be reasonable."

Dr. Barnabus was trying to make his voice soothing. It was then that I realized that this entire time, he had been using the more educated voice he had used on stage, rather than the rougher, lower-class voice he had used the first two times that we had met. Mr. Holmes had mentioned something like that right before I had been knocked out. Perhaps this Dr. Barnabus was of a higher class than he had pretended to be.

"What is she going to know that Holmes doesn't also know?" Johnson pointed out. "And I don't fancy having someone like Holmes on me. You've heard about all of his cases. He sniffs you out. I don't want him to be after us with a vengeance and with half of Scotland Yard because you got a little bloodthirsty."

"I wouldn't bother taking that tack with him," I said. "After all, he comes from a much higher-class family than you do. He could reconnect with them and they could help him get a lighter jail sentence. They could even quite him acquitted, should you all get arrested."

I wasn't sure how much of what I said was true. After all, Miss Bingley had been a rich woman of the high class and now she was facing the noose. However, I doubted that Johnson knew that.

Dr. Barnabus spluttered angrily while the thin man gaped at me, his mouth having dropped open.

Johnson squinted at me. "What do you know about it?"

His tone was not distrusting, but curious, and I knew that I had him.

"His clothes are of good quality and are the same material as this tent, which suggests that he once had access to a large income in order to buy all of that fabric. It's too expensive for someone of your background, and I apologize for my phrasing, but, well, I simply doubt that you could afford enough for the suit, never mind the amount needed to pay for the tent." I took a deep breath so that I would not stumble in my speech again. Now was not the time for my nerves to take over. "However, the suit was not made for him. It was made for someone similar in size and stature to him, so I would think a brother or a father. It is well-worn, as well, so something that had been used up and they no longer needed, something their sibling or child could easily beg from them. I would venture a guess that Dr. Barnabus, hardened criminal, is truly from the upper-middle-class at the least and merely pretends to be on the same class level as you in order to fit in better. Where else do you think his innate need for control came from? Or that accent?"

Johnson studied Dr. Barnabus as if seeing him for the first time.

The thin man jumped up. "She's right!" he whispered. He clearly stood next to Johnson and leaned in towards him a little as he spoke. "He'll get off easy if we kill her and we're caught. Even if he is the ringleader."

"We're not doing this," Johnson growled. "It's too great a risk. So far, we've just held her for a little bit. That's not too bad. She's not got a scratch on her. But murder? We'll be hanged for sure, and you'll be going free thanks to your rich family."

I did not think that Dr. Barnabus had been in contact with his family for some time. I suspected that he had stolen the suit and the tent, which had probably been designed for an outdoor family garden party or something of the kind. If he had been in contact, I doubt that he would have kept the same suit, despite it matching the tent, and would have found a way to acquire a newer suit for the occasion. But it didn't matter what the truth was, as much as it pained me to say it. I am usually all for saying the truth and for exposing the truth. It was part of why I was so excited to join up with Mr. Holmes. But my life was on the line and Mr. Holmes was nowhere in sight, probably dealing with his own troubles, and so I allowed myself to let Johnson and the other man believe whatever they wanted about Dr. Barnabus so long as it would save my life.

"You can't do this!" Dr. Barnabus spluttered. He looked rather red in the face. I doubted that many people had stood up to him and told him no over the course of his life.

"There's two of us," Johnson pointed out, quite rightly. "And only one of you. And we're the better fighters. 'You go and fight, Johnson,' you'd always say. 'I'm the brains and you're the brawn.'"

"Perhaps I have said that," Dr. Barnabus said, "but that doesn't mean that I don't know how to fight or that I can't hold my own against you two."

Johnson gave him a sharp grin. "We'll find out in just a moment, won't we?"

I had no wish to watch a violent fight break out, as much as I desired my freedom, but I was saved from having to witness such a thing because at that moment, there was the sound of many tramping feet and yells of "Police!" and "Scotland Yard!" and "Hold!"

I felt nearly faint with relief as the tent flap was yanked back and several policemen entered, brandishing their batons. I was sure that if I had been standing, I would have fallen from the way my legs felt like jelly.

One of the policemen rushed over to me and began to help me out of my bonds. "How on earth did you find me?" I asked, but I suspected that I already knew what the answer would be.

"Mr. Holmes dispatched us to you while he dealt with the disturbance in his apartment," the officer replied. "You're quite lucky, miss, that we got here in time."

I wanted to say that they hadn't gotten here in time at all and that I had managed to stall everything so that I was still alive by the time the police got there, but that wasn't very grateful of me. I knew that it could have gone so much worse, and that although the police hadn't been there to spare me trying to bargain for my life, at least they were here now and I could relax.

Dr. Barnabus was shooting daggers at me as he was loaded up into a police carriage. A part of me felt like waving at him just to be impudent, but I was quite exhausted and I didn't want to tempt fate by having a would-be murderer even angrier with me than before. Instead I merely thanked the police officers, and when asked, told them I'd like to be taken to 221B Baker Street.

There were other policemen milling about as I arrived, but they appeared to be in the process of dispersing. I was left to myself as I made my way up the steps to Mr. Holmes' flat. When I opened the door, my first urge was to laugh.

To anyone else looking at the mess, or indeed if the mess had been in anyone else's home, I would have known at once that someone had been burgled or suffered a similar sort of fate. Right now, though, to me it simply looked like Mr. Holmes was having a slightly more distracted day than usual. Papers were strewn everywhere, there was a poker lying on the floor, and there were a few broken dishes on the floor in the kitchen.

"It seems that a great row went on in here," I observed.

"I must say that it does not take great powers of observation to figure that out," Mr. Holmes replied.

He was sitting in his favorite chair and looked quite exhausted. I hoped that he was all right.

He immediately waved my concern away, observant as always and able to read me like an illustrated book. "Rest assured, Miss Bennet, I am well. I was rather more worried about yourself."

A felt a spike of anger. "I should think so, seeing as you left me with those men while you dashed off to your flat."

It felt as though all the anger I should have been feeling upon realizing that Mr. Holmes had abandoned me had merely been lying in wait until I was back with him in person again and was now making itself known in full force.

"I had no choice," Mr. Holmes said. "If the other half of Dr. Barnabus's team had accessed all of my case files and notes, they would have learned not only about all of my clients, whom I try to keep confidential, but about those I care about and wish to protect."

I could see his reasoning, but I still felt anger at his words. "Am I not someone you wish to protect?" I asked.

I had liked to think that we were becoming friends. Was that not the case?

Mr. Holmes turned to me with a look of astonishment. "Of course. But I could not be in two places at once and I had faith that you could handle yourself until Scotland Yard arrived. Did you not feel you were up to the task?"

I wanted to say that I didn't think I was up to the task at all and that I had, in fact, nearly gotten myself murdered. But a more reckless, selfish part of me was reveling in the fact that Mr. Holmes had invested enough trust in me to think that I could handle Dr. Barnabus and his hired men until Scotland Yard could arrive to take care of the rest. "I suppose that I was up to it, since I started them fighting amongst themselves and that delayed them long enough for the police to get there."

"You see then," Mr. Holmes said, as though that explained everything.

That was not, however, everything. Far from it. "Mr. Holmes," I said, "you must hear what happened, and not for the sake of my discussing my own actions, but for what I was told."

I relayed to him the mysterious employer that Dr. Barnabus mentioned and that this man, whoever he was, wanted information on Mr. Holmes and didn't want Mr. Holmes to know him personally.

When I had finished, Mr. Holmes sat silently for a long while. Finally, he said, "I am not sure what to make of this. I know that I have not always delivered a satisfactory answer to clients. It has always been a true answer and one that aligns with the facts, but that does not mean that it makes them happy. Truth and what someone wants do not always align. In fact, they align far more rarely than I would like. But I do not know of any former client who would be so dissatisfied with me that he would seek to plot against me in such a mysterious manner. This puzzle stumps me and I shall have to think on the matter further."

He then turned and looked at me. "And you should probably go home, Miss Bennet. You have been through quite a lot. It is time for me to think alone for now."

I knew that it was not so much my own condition as his desire to be alone that was why Mr. Holmes said that. He had happily ignored my exhaustion, my rumbling stomach, and any number of other things in the past because it suited him. He only acknowledged my exhaustion now because he wanted to. But at the moment, it was enough that he even saw that I was exhausted at all, whether he acknowledged it or not.

"I am rather glad you saw the chloroform coming," I said. "I assume that you realized what was going to happen and fought them off before they could dose you. But how did you know?"

"When I realized that this was not a real case and that it was all for show," Mr. Holmes explained. "I realized it in much the same way that you did. Once I knew that it was all for show, I knew that it must be a trap, and I moved."

I nodded. As always, Mr. Holmes was one step ahead of me. I looked forward to the day when our steps would be side by side. "Goodnight, Mr. Holmes."

He was back to staring at the fire. "Goodnight, Miss Bennet."

# CHAPTER EIGHT:
## Family Matters

All the way home, I contemplated what had happened that day. I had been in danger. I had been alone. My life had nearly been taken from me and it had been only my wit that had saved me. If the police hadn't come, I might still be dead, or Johnson and his compatriot could have beaten Dr. Barnabus into submission and I would have been spared but much more shaken than I already was.

Did I really want to continue working with Mr. Holmes, seeing firsthand the kind of danger he brought to him? I had thought of him initially as the kind of man who dispelled danger. He took something mysterious and upsetting like murder and he explained how it had happened and he helped to catch the offender. Now I was seeing the opposite, how his mission to bring people to justice could be used against him. Mr. Holmes loved puzzles and the promise of a good one would be too much for him to resist. It was likely that we could both end up in a similar situation again.

But I couldn't give up what I had discovered. I couldn't. I loved the adventure and being treated as an equal. I loved helping people. I loved putting the pieces together and using my observational skills and pushing my mind to the limit. And as much as I sometimes wanted to beat him over the head with his own moldy food, I enjoyed the company of Mr. Holmes over the company of most other society. With Charlotte gone to live as Mrs. Collins at Rosings and Jane distracted by her own life as mistress of a house and with a baby on the way, who else was left to me but Mr. Holmes?

But if I was resolved to keep working with Mr. Holmes, then I must inform my family of the truth.

It was my near brush with death that solidified this for me. If something were to happen to me, I didn't want to simply vanish into the fog. I didn't want to be a mystery to my parents. I didn't want them to despair and hope in turn, wondering if I might come back alive, and I didn't want them to learn about any sad ends I had reached through sensational newspapers or gossip. I wanted them to know what I was up to and be aware in case the worst should happen.

A part of me felt that my mother, especially, should continue to live in ignorant bliss. But wouldn't that make the blow all the harder when it fell? And she should probably start giving up her dreams of my marrying sooner rather than later. I doubted at this point that I would marry at all. It was certainly not what I sought out of life anymore, not that I had sought it out too hard to begin with.

It was only fair to them, as Mr. Bingley had pointed out. They were my family. At the end of the day, they cared about me and they deserved to know.

I arrived home to find a very anxious Jane and Mr. Bingley awaiting me. The moment she saw my face, Jane burst out. "My dear Lizzie, what on earth?"

I realized that I had quite forgotten about my disguise. Part of it had come off in the process of getting me bound to the chair, I am sure, but parts of it were still in place and I still wore the outfit I had put on for that purpose. My original dress was still back at Mr. Holmes' flat. I would have to fetch it in the morning.

"I had a delightful time with Mr. Holmes," I said.

I hated that I was lying, but even though I was about to be honest with the rest of my family regarding my general activities with Mr. Holmes, I was not about to reveal to Jane or anyone else exactly what had happened. There was no need to give them cause for concern after the cause had already passed.

"We went to a costume party of sorts," I continued. "I hope that I haven't worried you. It was rather last-minute and we had just made up after a bit of a disagreement."

"We were worried," Jane admitted, "but I am always worried when you are with Mr. Holmes."

Mr. Bingley was standing off to the side and wisely chose to exit the room.

I sat down on the edge of the lounge, at Jane's knees. "Mr. Holmes always takes pains to keep me perfectly safe," I said.

It was an exaggeration, but he had taken care in his own way. He had put me in disguise, and sent the police to rescue me. Coming from someone as generally thoughtless as Mr. Holmes, it was exceedingly thoughtful.

"I am sure that he does," Jane said, "and you know that Charles thinks highly of him. There is just so much going on in London all the time. It feels as though every day I hear another gruesome tale. It is not at all like home, where you could go walking for miles and be perfectly all right. I remember you would vanish for whole afternoons and come back with the hem of your dress caked in mud and soaked right through."

I laughed. I remembered that as well. I loved walking. It was one of my greatest pleasures at home besides reading. Mother was often in despair over the state of my dress and would cluck and ask what if I arrived at a gentleman's house in such a state?

That reminded me of my final purpose for the evening. "Jane," I said, "Charles has told me about your plans to invite our other sisters up to London."

"I thought it would be good for them," Jane replied. "For different reasons, of course. And then they can hopefully be here for the birth of the baby, even if they cannot stay on as you are."

"You mean for them to see the joys of childbirth?" I teased. Jane and I had heard many horrid tales of how the birthing of a child went.

Jane laughed. "You are mischievous." Then she sobered. "Of course, we will try to keep your activities just between us, but you know how inquisitive they all are."

"I understand," I said. "And I shall speak with them when they arrive in person. But I was thinking that I would write to Mother and tell her about it."

Jane did her best to sit up, so great was her surprise. I had to coax her back down. "Are you serious, Lizzie? I know that you have kept a great deal of your heart from Mother, and I think you've had reason to. I had hoped that you would confide this matter to her but I had not expected it. I am quite pleased, you have no idea. It is so much better for her to hear it from you than from one of the other girls."

And it was so much better for her to hear it from me and not from a newspaper, but I did not say that part out loud. There was no reason to make Jane worried. Not with the baby so near its time. "I'm going to go and write to her now, if that's all right with you."

"Of course!" Jane raised her voice. "Charles?"

Mr. Bingley appeared almost as if by magic, and I suspected him of listening by the door in case he needed to intervene. "Yes, darling?"

Jane waved at me and I realized she was indicating that I should speak my plans aloud. "I am going to write to my mother and tell her of my activities. I agree with you that it's only right that she hear it from me. My father already has a good idea of my mind and I think will be able to help soothe her in time for when I next see them in person."

"Hopefully it will prevent her from murdering you and Mr. Holmes having to solve who did it," Mr. Bingley teased.

"I'm afraid in that case it shall be rather obvious," I said, "for Mother was never one for being subtle."

As Mr. Bingley well knew, having experienced her in a social situation where her daughter could possibly marry an eligible bachelor, namely Mr. Bingley.

I rose. "I shall go and write, then, and I think I shall turn in early. I am quite exhausted." This was true. I could feel exhaustion starting to creep in, and suddenly the last thing that I wanted to do was be in the presence of other people.

Jane and Mr. Bingley let me go with quiet loving murmurs, and I let myself walk slowly up to my room without rushing. The ordeals of the day were catching up with me. I had to force myself to sit at the desk instead of sinking right into a bath and then into bed.

I stared at the pieces of paper in front of me for a much longer time than I'd like to admit. My mother and I had never been close. Kitty and Lydia had been her darlings. From the start, my father and I had an affinity, a kind of kindred touch with one another, but Mother and I had forever been at odds. I know that she often despaired of Mary and me making matches. How was I supposed to broach the matter of such a delicate and important subject to her?

Finally, I decided to simply go with the only thing that I knew, the thing that was important to me and part of why I had joined with Mr. Holmes: the truth. The knowledge that I had come so close to never writing her again spurred me on. If a near-death experience was not enough to provoke honesty, then what was?

*Dear Mother,*

*I apologize in my lack of writing to you. I hope to do more in the future. Please give my love to Papa and Mary and tell Mary that I look forward to seeing her when she and Kitty and Lydia come to stay in London. Jane and I are most anxious for them, especially Jane, who has grown quite frustrated with her state. She and Mr. Bingley send their love to all of you, as well.*

*I have to tell you that I am not only writing to convey my love. I have important news to tell you. I have delayed in the telling because I know that it will upset you and I don't wish to do that, as much as you may talk of my living only to unsettle your nerves.*

*You may well remember the Mr. Holmes who helped in the unfortunate matter with Mr. Wickham. I have found myself quite excited at my own part in helping him, and since I am in London with*

*Jane, I have taken the liberty of calling on him. He treats me as an equal and through him I have been learning how to solve cases as he does. It has been wildly exciting and I wish that you could feel as I do when I have helped to solve a case and bring peace to an unhappy person. There is no feeling as good in the world, I think, as that feeling.*

*I hope that this does not upset you unduly. I know that it is not ladylike and not what you wanted for your daughter. But it is what makes me happy. I feel useful and like my mind is finally being put to a good use. Perhaps in time you can understand. I am helping people and doing something with my life, and doing it with someone who treats me as though I am truly someone, a person, and not just a dancing partner. He treats me as Papa does, only less of the fatherly way about him, of course.*

*I am happy to answer any questions that you may have. And while you might not believe it, given what I have just told you, Mama, I do love you.*

*Sincerely,*
*Lizzie*

I closed and sealed the letter and then finally got myself a nice hot bath. As I relaxed and let the aches and fears of the day slide away, the letter weighed on my mind. The idea of this mysterious person after Mr. Holmes weighed on me. My sisters approaching and what they would think of me weighed on me. My future and what it would hold and what dangers I might yet come across weighed on me.

There was only one way to see any of these things resolved, I decided.

I must wait and see.

**THE END**

# *ABOUT THE AUTHOR:*

## *Amelia Littlewood*

Amelia works as a librarian and lives in an idyllic Cotswold village in England with Darcy, her Persian cat. She has been a Jane Austen fan since childhood but only in later life did she discover the glory and gory of a cozy mystery book. She has drafted many different cases for Holmes and Bennet to solve together.

Visit www.amelialittlewood.com for more details

# *AMELIA LITTLEWOOD:*

## *Interview*

***How did you find yourself writing a book? What's the story behind your career?***

My passion for books started at a very young age and has only grown as I've got older. I found myself jotting ideas down for stories in my spare time, using inspiration from books I was reading at the time. I've always been a fan of Sherlock Holmes and love a good mystery, but my other great love is anything Jane Austen. I was reading Pride and Prejudice and started thinking, what if these two characters were around at the same time?

How would they interact? What adventures would they go on? Holmes and Bennet are both intellectual characters, both observant, quick witted and independent. The meeting of minds could be quite good fun.

***What do you think of the writing world? Are you happy being part of it?***

Working as a librarian, I've seen the writing world change so much over the years. There are so many people who have been able to self publish their work who wouldn't otherwise have been accepted. Some may not see this as a good thing, but I feel if people are inspired to write and come together on social media to support each other on their literary journeys, it can only be a good thing. I'm enjoying being part of this new wave of authors, but am also lucky enough to have support from my Publisher.

***What is it about Pride and Prejudice, and Sherlock Holmes that you find interesting?***

Both books and both characters allow for pure escapism! I love both time periods, with their period dress, etiquette and simplicity. Elizabeth and Sherlock, although from different time periods, are both very similar in the fact they are independent people. They question the restraints of their worlds and are brave enough to be themselves. I can imagine the intrigue and admiration they would have for each other if they met, which leads to an interesting connection in my books.

*What makes your books interesting?*

Not many authors want to tackle mixing two characters from different time zones, but I felt this could be quite good fun?! So, why not?! We have an instant connection to both of the characters which makes the books easy quick reads to slot into our busy lifestyles when we get a minute or two to relax.

*Who are your favourite authors?*

Jane Austen, of course. And, Sir Arthur Conan Doyle. I also enjoy T E Kinsey, Cee Cee James as well as classics by Agatha Christie.

*How much time do you spend writing?*

It seems to be most of the time at the moment! I spend most weekends writing, as well as lunch breaks and some evenings. I try to get a few hundred words down every day, even if they get edited out, it's still progress. I also carry a notepad with me and scribble the odd idea, phrase, or thought as I get them.

*What are you reading right now?*

I'm currently working my way through M C Beaton's Agatha Raisin series. I live in the Cotswolds so recognize some of the locations used in the books.

*Do you have a set writing schedule?*

I'm aiming to write one book a month, each about 20,000 words long. I have lots of ideas that I want to add to the Holmes and Bennet series. I made a conscious decision to write short stories to satisfy the "quick fix" that readers need in their busy schedule. Most people are working full time, juggling running a house, or arranging time around children, so if they get time to read it's generally half an hour before bed. What I wanted to do was to produce stories that you can read in their entirety while you're eating your lunch, or waiting in the dentists.

*What has been the biggest thrill of your writing career so far?*

Holding copies of my own books in my hands, signing them and giving a copy each to my grandparents and parents. They have been so supportive and are really proud.

***What other creative outlets do you have?***

I love to sew. Last year I made some little Christmas decorations and gave them away as presents to my family and friends. I also love baking and trying new recipes, and have even been known to host the odd dinner party with invites, decorations and activities inspired by creative things people have made on Pinterest.

***What are your three favourite movies?***

I love 'About Time'. Bill Nighy is excellent, as always. This film has such a lovely message about enjoying every moment in our lives, and looking for the good in everything.

Another, which is not really a film, but a true masterpiece, is the BBC's version of 'Pride and Prejudice'. I have watched this so many times and never tire of it. Colin Firth is the best Mr. Darcy in my opinion.

When I need cheering up and need something to enjoy with a group of friends and a glass of wine, we go for films like 'The Heat' with Sandra Bullock.

# JANE AUSTEN:
## A Biography

An English novelist, Jane Austen became famous posthumously for her books which outlined and challenged life during the 19th century. She became influential in changing the way novels were written, and was respected for her ability to portray the depth of her characters' emotions. Her stories were accurate examples of middle-class life in England during the era. The books also sympathized with women and their need to rely on men, at the time, for economic security and social standing. The irony and realism with which Austen wrote, resulted in the novels becoming classics and are responsible for the extent to which they have been studied and published.

### *The Author's Early Life*

Jane Austen was born on December 16, 1775 in Steventon, Hampshire, England. She was her parent's seventh child, and their second daughter. Along with her siblings, Jane grew up in an environment that encouraged learning and creative thinking. The local Anglican priest and an avid scholar, Austen's father had an extensive library and all the children were encouraged to peruse the books daily. Jane and her sister were sent to boarding schools, to allow the girls the opportunity to acquire a more formal education, during their preadolescent years. They had to return home, however, due to financial constraints and the acquisition of typhus, which almost resulted in Jane's death.

### *The Progression of Austen's Literary Works*

Austen's entire family had a love of reading and acting, and the children would put on plays for family and friends. Her father encouraged Jane to write, despite how unconventional this would have been at the time. He bought expensive writing and drawing materials for Jane and Cassandra. She began to write short stories, poems and plays in bound notebooks during the 1790s. Scholars have perused the writings in these notebooks, which are now referred to as Jane's *Juvenilia*.

Austen began writing her *Juvenilia* from the age of 11, predominantly for the family's entertainment. The plots included an exaggeration of everyday life, and fantasies of females that would take more power within their own lives. The writings were done between 1787 and 1793, and consisted of three compilations, made by Austen in her later years: *Volume the First*, *Volume the Second*, and *Volume the Third*. One of the stories which stood out the most was a satirical novella, outlined in letters called *Love and Friendship.* Austen wrote the story at the age of 14, and based the storyline on mocking novels of sensibility.

Another notable piece within the compilation was *The History of England*, which was a 34 page parody of historical writing that included illustrations by Cassandra. Jane began writing longer stories, after the *Juvenilia*, completing *Lady Susan* between 1793 and 1795. The way in which the novella was written differed from her other work, based on the characters' personalities. Reviewers have described the heroine as a sexual predator, who uses her intelligence and charm to manipulate her lovers and friends.

After completing *Lady Susan*, Austen began her first full-length novel, *Elinor and Marianne.* This book was later published anonymously, as

*Sense and Sensibility,* with *by a Lady* appearing on the title page instead of the author's name. The story was told through a series of letters, and follows the lives of two sisters, Elinor (19) and Marianne (16½) as they come of age. They undertake a journey from their childhood estate to a new home, along with their widowed mother and younger sister, Margaret. Austen successfully brings across the emotions of the women, through love, seduction and heartache.

All of Austen's novels were read to her family intermittently during their evolution, and she began reading her second novel, *First Impressions* (published as *Pride and Prejudice*), to them in 1796. The initial draft was completed by August of the following year. This was the family's 'established favorite' and her father (possibly unknown to Jane) made an attempt at getting it published, which was declined. Upon its completion, Austen wrote her third novel, *Susan* (better known as *Northanger Abbey*) and her father sold the copyright to Benjamin Crosby, a London publisher, for £10. Crosby promised early publication, which he never fulfilled, and Austen repurchased the copyright from him in 1816 and got the novel published elsewhere.

Neither Austen sister ever got married, and they moved to Bath with their parents in 1801, after their father retired. He unexpectedly died from an illness in 1805, leaving the girls and their mother in financial difficulty. While the family lived in Bath, the amount of writing that Jane did significantly dwindled. Historians have suggested that the new environment may have led to a form of depression, resulting in writer's block. It was also in Bath that Jane received her only known marriage proposal. She accepted at first, but decided against it the following morning. In a letter to her niece, Austen advised getting married to somebody for love, not status, stating that 'anything is to be preferred or endured rather than marrying without affection.'

After her father's death, the three women moved around for a period, visiting family and renting short term lodgings, before settling at her brother's cottage in Chawton. Jane was now in her 30s and, going through her brother Henry, began to publish her novels anonymously. Henry made arrangements with Thomas Egerton to publish *Sense and Sensibility* first, which was released in October 1811. It was well received, especially by young aristocratic opinion-makers. The first edition of the novel sold out by mid-1813, and a second edition was printed shortly after. With the publication of her first book, Austen received a sense of financial independence and security.

Egerton went on to publish *Pride and Prejudice* and *Mansfield Park,* in January 1813 and May 1814, respectively. Both novels were popular with the public and, without the author's knowledge, were translated and published in France. Austen's novels also became favorites of the Prince Regent and he requested a meeting with the author. At his librarian's suggestion, Austen dedicated her next publication, *Emma*, to the Prince Regent; although she secretly resented all the advice his librarian had offered.

In 1815, Austen changed her publisher to John Murray, who had a better reputation in London than Egerton. He was responsible for releasing *Emma* in December 1815, and a second edition of *Mansfield Park* in 1816. As with all Austen's new novels, *Emma* was well received but the profits were offset by how poorly the second edition did. These novels were her final books to be published during Jane Austen's lifetime. While alive, she sadly never received the credit she deserved as an author.

### *Austen's Decline in Health and Death*

By 1816, Austen began to have health problems which continued to escalate throughout the year. It is now believed that she had been suffering with Addison's disease, although this may not have been acknowledged at the time. She continued to write throughout most of her illness, only putting down her pen on March 18, 1817. As her physical decline continued, Austen became extremely lethargic and was confined to bed a month later. By

May she was in incredible pain and, reportedly, longing for the release of death. Her closest siblings, Henry and Charlotte, registered her in a home in Winchester for treatment, where she died on July 18, 1817. Austen was buried in Winchester Cathedral, with an epitaph that makes no mention of her writing skills.

### *Jane Austen's Legacy*

After her death, Cassandra and Henry published her final two novels, *Persuasion* and *Northanger Abbey*, as a set. Henry Austen added a *Bibliographical Note,* which identified Jane Austen as the author of all the books she had written. Today, her novels are continuously read and studied worldwide. They have been reviewed academically and are considered to be among the classics from the 19th century.

Austen was voted as number 70 on the BBC's list of '100 Most Famous Britons of All Time.' Her novels have been adapted into various films and TV shows which include: *Emma, Mansfield Park, Sense and Sensibility,* and *Pride and Prejudice. Emma* was also the inspiration for the film Clueless. Although she didn't received the credit she deserved during her lifetime, Austen continues to inspire readers, scholars and writers centuries after her books were first anonymously published. She is a testimony to the way thinking and times change, in both novels and in real life.

# *ARTHUR CONAN DOYLE:*

## *Literary Genius, Honorable Man*

Best known for his Sherlock Holmes stories, Arthur Conan Doyle became a literary legend in the late 19$^{th}$ century. The author was born in Edinburgh, Scotland on May 22, 1859 to Charles and Mary Doyle. His father was a moderately successful artist, from a wealthy background, and his mother's incredible story telling ability became one of the major influences behind Doyle's writing. He expresses his fondness for her in his autobiography, and the motivation her constant support inspired.

### Education and Early Influences

After an offer from his extended family when Doyle was nine, the author was sent to a Jesuit boarding school in England. His memoirs indicate that the seven years he spent here were filled with corporal punishment and bigotry, which went against the morals that Doyle placed value upon. To deal with the unhappy environment, he began to play sports and write to his mother regularly. He would also thrill his school mates with brilliant tales, that he would dictate to small gatherings several evenings per week. Despite the horrors of his school life, Doyle was resilient, and graduated at the age of 17 'wild, full-blooded and a trifle reckless.'

Ready to face the world and determined to be successful because of his mother's ongoing support, Doyle was first faced with the daunting task of institutionalising his father. Charles' alcoholism had gotten out of control during his son's absence, and his mental health had deteriorated to match. Doyle described the circumstances of his father's breakdown and institutionalisation in his 1880 story, *The Surgeon of Gaston Fell.*

Influenced greatly by the lodger his mother took in after, Dr. Brian Waller, Doyle decided to become a physician. He enrolled in the University of Edinburgh, the same place where Waller had gone to school. Here he met several other future authors, including Robert Louis Stevenson, who was also studying at the time.

The inspiration for his Sherlock Homes character came in the form of one of Doyle's teachers, Dr. Joseph Bell. The doctor was skilled in observation, logic, deduction and diagnosis, all of which became key traits of Holmes' personality. After attending university for a couple years, Doyle wrote his first story, T*he Mystery of Sasassa Valley*, which was taken by the Edinburgh magazine *Chamber's Journal*. He also published another story that year, *An American Tale*, this time accepted by *London Society*.

In his 20$^{th}$ year, Doyle received an offer to become a ship's surgeon aboard *The Hope*, a whaling boat about to set sail for the Arctic. He accepted and, despite the brutality he observed while the crew was hunting for seals, thoroughly enjoyed the experience. He later said; it awakened in him the need for adventure and the soul of a wanderer. As with many of the momentous events in his life, the journey was described in one of his stories, *A Captain of the Pole-Star*.

After his sea adventure, Doyle returned to his studies and graduated in 1881 with a Bachelor of Medicine and Master of Surgery degree.

### *Professional Doctor and Aspiring Author*

After his graduation, Arthur Conan Doyle accepted another offer aboard a vessel scheduled to sail between Liverpool and Africa, *The Mayumba.* Not enjoying the journey as much as he had on The Hope, he relinquished his position upon its return to England. He then worked for a brief period with an immoral doctor in Plymouth. This experience is described in detail in *The Stark Munro Letters,* published many years later.

Ambition caused Doyle to move to Portsmouth where he opened his first practice. Within three years the doctor had become well established in the community, due to his compassion and hardworking nature. He also continued writing, pursuing his dream of becoming an established author. In August 1885, Doyle married his first wife, the gentle, amiable Louisa Hawkins.

### *Sherlock Holmes and the Supernatural*

In 1888, a story which had been revised and the title changed, introduced the world to Sherlock Holmes and Dr. Watson. *A Study in Scarlet*, was published in the *Beeton's Christmas Annual,* and the characters propelled him to immediate success. Doyle, however, began to resent the popularity of the Holmes stories as he believed that they were a distraction from those he really wanted recognition for, such as historical novels, poems and plays.

Despite the success of Holmes and the birth of his daughter, Mary, Doyle was becoming restless and moved to Vienna to specialise in ophthalmology. When this did not prove to be feasible, the family returned to London and Doyle opened another practice in Upper Wimpole Street. With no patients and lots of time to spare, he began writing a short series featuring Sherlock Holmes. His agent, A.P. Watt, signed a deal with *The Strand* for all the stories to be published in the magazine.

In May 1891, Doyle developed a near fatal case of influenza. After recovering, he decided to abandon his medical career and pursue his writing full-time. His frustrations with Holmes began to grow, and in 1893, the author wrote a story in which Holmes plunged to his death. It is reported that 20,000 Strand customers cancelled their subscriptions in protest. Doyle then began a period of intense writing, determined to prove his skills beyond Sherlock Holmes.

In 1892, his wife had given birth to their son, Kingsley, which Doyle described as the chief event in their life together. His immersion in writing, however, caused him to overlook her deteriorating health. Louisa was diagnosed with tuberculosis, and given only a few months to live in 1893. Doyle tended to her personally, causing her lifespan to extend many years beyond this prediction.

In the late 1880s, Doyle had developed an interest in the paranormal and spirituality. This inspired him to write *The Mystery of Cloomber*, a story about three vengeful Buddhist monks. With Louisa's death looming over them, the author's fascination with the life beyond increased. He joined The Society for Psychical Research and became very vocal about his spiritual beliefs. Louisa passed away in her husband's arms on July 4, 1906, after which Doyle fell into a deep depression.

### *War and Psychic Journeys*

Doyle attempted to enlist in the army during The Boer War, but his application was rejected as he was already 40 and slightly overweight. This did not stop him from being a part of the war, however, as he volunteered as a doctor and sailed to Africa in February 1900. There he witnessed more soldiers and medical staff die of typhoid fever, than war wounds. *The Great Boer War* was a result of this time served, and is a masterpiece that gave many details about the war that would otherwise have remained hidden. In 1902, King Edward VII knighted Doyle for the services he rendered to the crown, during the war.

Even though his high moral values meant that Doyle had remained faithful to his wife after she had gotten sick, he had met and fallen in love with Jean Beckie in 1897. The pair remained close friends and got married on September 18, 1907. They moved to Sussex, with his two children, and settled here for the rest of their lives. They added three more children to their family, Denis (1909), Adrian (1910) and Jean (1912).

Having written many war stories and with the keen observation skills of a writer, Doyle was able to predict WWI and sent articles to several newspapers advising that the country get 'military ready' before it began. He also foresaw the possibility of blockades created by enemy submarines and suggested building a canal. Unfortunately, his public warnings were dismissed as 'ramblings' by the navy and they ignored his advice. After the war began, 55-year-old Doyle once again tried to enlist and was rejected. Not to be denied the opportunity to serve his country, he organised a civilian battalion which had over 100 volunteers.

The war caused the author to lose many people close to him, including his son, brother, nephew and two brothers-in-law. These deaths increased Doyle's need to learn more about spirituality and the possibility of life after death. Despite the mocking of the press and the church's disapproval, he continued to research and talk about the occult. His wife shared his beliefs, and developed the ability to 'trance-write.' Most his work became about the supernatural and spirituality, and the entire family took trips abroad on psychic crusades.

Despite being diagnosed with Angina Pectoris, Doyle insisted on taking a final psychic tour in Europe. Upon his return, he was in so much pain that he had to be carried ashore. The adventurer in him would not allow Doyle to remain bedridden, however, and on a cold spring day in 1930 he managed to walk unseen into the garden. He was later found with one hand clutching his heart, and the other holding a single snowdrop. Arthur Conan Doyle died on March 7, 1930, surrounded by his family. The last words the author said before he departed for 'the greatest and most glorious adventure of all,' were whispered to his wife, 'You are wonderful.'

www.ingramcontent.com/pod-product-compliance
Lightning Source LLC
Chambersburg PA
CBHW030518310726
48979CB00010B/1713/J

* 9 7 8 1 9 9 9 7 6 0 0 6 9 *